The Amazing Panda Adventure

Books by Todd Strasser

The Amazing Panda Adventure

A novelization by Todd Strasser
Based on the
Screenplay by Jeff Rothberg and Laurice Elehwany
Story by John Wilcox & Steven Alldredge

SCHOLASTIC INC.
New York Toronto London Auckland Sydney

WARNER BROS. PRESENTS

A LEE RICH/GARY FOSTER PRODUCTION A CHRISTOPHER CAIN FILM "THE AMAZING PANDA ADVENTURE"
STEPHEN LANG YI DING RYAN SLATER MUSIC BY WILLIAM ROSS EXECUTIVE PRODUCER GABRIELLA MARTINELLI
STORY BY JOHN WILCOX & STEVEN ALLDREDGE SCREENPLAY BY JEFF ROTHBERG AND LAURICE ELEHWANY
PRODUCED BY LEE RICH, JOHN WILCOX, GARY FOSTER AND DYLAN SELLERS
DIRECTED BY CHRISTOPHER CAIN

PG PARENTAL GUIDANCE SUGGESTED
SOME MATERIAL MAY NOT BE SUITABLE FOR CHILDREN

WARNER BROS. FAMILY ENTERTAINMENT
A TIME WARNER ENTERTAINMENT COMPANY

ISBN 0-590-55205-8

12 11 10 9 8 7 6 5 4 3 2   5 6 7 8 9/9 0/0

Printed in the U.S.A.   40

First Scholastic printing, August 1995

1

The classroom was hot, the air stuffy. Ryan Tyler's collar felt tight. If there was one thing he really hated, it was standing up in front of the class and talking. But that's what he was doing. Other kids didn't have to do it. Today was Fathers' Career Day, and their fathers could stand up and speak for themselves. But Ryan's father wasn't there.

He was *never* there.

So Ryan had to get up in front of the class and present on Career Day himself. Ryan was twelve, and this was seventh grade. He had brown hair and was a little taller than most of the other guys, but not as tall as the tallest girls.

"The giant panda is the most famous animal in the world," he said, reading from a small stack of index cards in his trembling hands. "It is the international symbol for peace. Only there's no peace in its life. Pandas live in the mountain forests of western China. And because the forests are disappearing, so is the panda. Today there are fewer than one thousand pandas left in the world. But the panda's biggest threat to extinction isn't only the forests, it's also that people just don't care."

Ryan paused to catch his breath and to make sure that his last point really sank in. His teacher, Mrs. Nash, smiled and nodded approvingly. About two thirds of the kids in the class were staring out the window looking bored. The other third watched him and pretended to look interested, but only because they thought looking interested would impress Mrs. Nash and get them a higher grade.

Ryan took a deep breath and finished up. "And that's what my father does for a living. Right now he's in China fighting off lions and tigers and poachers to save pandas. Just like Indiana Jones. And that's why he's not here. Saving pandas is more important."

Mrs. Nash smiled approvingly and walked toward the front of the classroom. "Thank you, Ryan. That was very interesting."

Ryan breathed a sigh of relief and headed back toward his seat. Meanwhile, Mrs. Nash introduced the next speaker: "And now Johnny's father will speak about his chosen profession, the night shift at 7-Eleven."

Johnny Pratt was Ryan's best friend. He was a round-faced, short, pudgy kid with red hair and freckles. Mr. Pratt was basically a bigger version of Johnny. The kids in the class started to smirk as Mr. Pratt lumbered up to the blackboard. Ryan glanced at Johnny and saw that his face was red with embarrassment. After all, what could be interesting about working at 7-Eleven? But when Mr. Pratt started telling them about how many times he'd been held up at gunpoint, everyone got real quiet and interested. Not a single kid stared out the window.

Johnny glanced back at Ryan and gave him a smile and a wink. Ryan sighed and wished his father had been there to do the panda presentation. Surely he would have made the panda story more interesting. But as usual, his father had more important things to do.

"Actually, getting held up isn't the best part of my dad's job," Johnny was saying. School was over and he and Ryan were walking home along a tree-lined sidewalk. Ryan was wearing his Chicago Cubs baseball cap backward. Johnny was munching on a Ding Dong.

"The best part of my dad's job is when he brings home the Twinkies and all the other good stuff," Johnny went on.

"You mean, he steals it?" Ryan asked.

"Naw, he just waits until it's past the expiration date," Johnny explained.

"Aren't you worried that they're spoiled?" Ryan asked.

"No way," said Johnny. "Pop says there's enough chemicals in that stuff to choke a moose. But I guess workin' in the 7-Eleven is nothing compared to saving pandas."

Ryan just shrugged. "Saving pandas isn't such a big deal."

They continued down the sidewalk toward Ryan's house. As they got close, Johnny finished the Ding Dong and started eating a 3 Musketeers candy bar. Ryan lived in a small, gray, split-level house. The paint was starting to peel, but Ryan knew his mom couldn't afford to get it painted. They went up the front walk. Ryan stopped at the mailbox and took out the mail.

"Ask your mom if I can stay for dinner," Johnny said while Ryan shuffled through the letters.

"You stay every night," Ryan said without looking up.

"Yeah, but I don't want her to think I'm a mooch," Johnny said.

Ryan didn't answer. He was staring down at a letter he'd never expected to receive. Johnny pointed at the stamp with a finger smudged with melted chocolate. It was a picture of a panda's face. "What's that?"

"That's the symbol of the reserve where my dad works," Ryan said. "They call it a panda reserve."

"What's a reserve?" Johnny asked.

"It's a place where they protect animals," Ryan explained.

"Like a zoo?"

"No, it's much bigger," Ryan said. "Like thousands of square miles. It's all wild, protected land."

He pushed the front door open and shouted, "Hi, Mom!"

"Hi, sweetheart," his mother called back from the kitchen.

Keeping the letter from his dad, Ryan tossed the rest of the mail on the coffee table in the living room and then headed upstairs. Johnny was right on his heels. Just as he was about to reach for the banister Mrs. Tyler called out, "Johnny, don't get chocolate on my banister."

"How'd she know?" Johnny asked, wiping his hands on his shirt as he followed Ryan into his room.

"Believe me, it's easy," Ryan said, sitting down on the bed and tearing open the letter, which was thicker than the ones his father had sent in the past.

Dirty clothes were scattered around the floor, and the walls were covered with posters of baseball players and a Chicago Cubs baseball pennant. Johnny picked up a miniature basketball and shot it through the hoop hanging from Ryan's closet door while Ryan read.

"So what's your dad have to say?" Johnny asked

as Ryan pulled a set of airplane tickets out of the letter. "Hey, cool. Going somewhere?"

"China," Ryan replied, sort of stunned.

Johnny stopped shooting baskets and came over. "For real?"

Ryan nodded. "Over spring break."

"Excellent," Johnny said. "You can help your dad save a few pandas."

"I guess," Ryan replied. The thought of seeing his dad kindled a wide range of mixed emotions inside him.

"How long since you've seen him?"

"Not since the divorce," Ryan said. "Two years."

"Wow, that must be weird."

Beep! Beep! Beep! They were suddenly interrupted by the alarm on Ryan's watch.

"*American Gladiators!*" Johnny gasped and dashed for the TV room. Ryan dropped the letter and plane tickets on his bed and followed. China could wait.

In the lush green mountains of the Szechwan province of western China, in a vast reserve set up by the government for the protection of wild creatures, a full-grown female panda moved like a shadow through the thick, cool bamboo forest. An everpresent mist hung over the forest, which was dotted with tall evergreen trees, red birches, and magnolias. Higher up, the forest gave way to alpine meadows, and above that to barren cliffs and steep rock-strewn slides before ending at white snow-capped peaks.

The female panda walked carefully on three paws, as if the fourth was injured. But it wasn't. Instead, it cradled a newborn cub close to her side.

The cub was the most important thing not only in the female panda's life, but in the lives of many others as well. She didn't know that her cub was the only surviving newborn panda of that season. And because of that, the entire fate of the reserve, and all the creatures in it, depended on the cub's survival.

2

Spring recess had arrived, and with it, the trip Ryan had been dreading for weeks. Of course, he hadn't told anyone how much he dreaded it. You weren't supposed to refuse something as special as a trip to China. You weren't supposed to refuse the opportunity to see your father for the first time in two years.

It was two o'clock in the morning, and the flight was less than a dozen hours away. Ryan lay in his bed wide awake in his dark bedroom with a flashlight in his hands. The beam of light was aimed at the ceiling, which his father had long ago painted dark blue. Over the blue, he'd painted all the major constellations of stars in yellow. So that lying in bed was sort of like camping out and staring up at the stars.

Ryan looked up at them feeling a mixture of fear and sadness. Good-bye, Gemini, he thought. Good-bye, Orion, and good hunting. Good-bye, Big Dipper, don't spill anything while I'm gone.

Bye, Ursa Minor . . . Little Bear . . .

Ryan yawned and flicked off the flashlight. It was much too late and he had to get some sleep. Tomorrow he would begin a trip that would take more than twenty-four hours to complete.

Halfway around the world, deep in the panda reserve, Ryan's father, Dr. Michael Tyler, crept through the underbrush of vines and bamboo shoots, following a fifteen-year-old Chinese girl named Ling.

"Well?" Michael whispered.

"Close, I think," Ling whispered back.

"You *think*?" Michael repeated, slightly annoyed.

"Many go their whole life without seeing a panda in the wild," Ling replied quietly.

"Well, if we don't see one soon, it's going to be too late."

"Shhh!" Ling held a finger to her lips and pointed ahead. Michael crawled up beside her and squinted. Through a thick patch of bamboo he could see a clearing.

"Listen," Ling whispered.

Michael held his breath and heard a faint crunching sound. A chill ran through him. He'd heard the sound before in zoos and in the enclosures back at the reserve headquarters. It was the sound of a panda grinding mature bamboo in its powerful jaws. Few creatures in the world had jaws powerful enough, or a stomach tough enough, to consume nearly rock-hard bamboo.

Ling started to crawl foward and Michael followed. Despite being more than twice her age, he trusted her completely. At fifteen, Ling knew the forest better than he would ever know it.

Once again, Ling stopped. This time she reached for a long narrow tube she carried in her day pack. Michael knew at once what that meant. He stopped and waited while Ling pressed one end of the tube to her lips and aimed.

Ffftttt. . . . The sound of her exhaling broke the silence. It was followed by a startled yelp and a soft scraping sound, as if something were trying to drag itself across the ground. Finally, Michael heard a thud.

Ling turned toward him and nodded. Then she quickly stood and went forward through the undergrowth. Dr. Tyler stood up and followed. Ahead he caught a glimpse of something black and white lying on the ground. They'd gotten one!

She was a full-grown female, probably close to three hundred pounds, lying on her stomach with her legs splayed out like a huge stuffed bear. Michael quickly pulled off his pack and took out a camera as well as a chart and tape measure. He photographed and measured her, then checked her ears and eyes. Meanwhile, Ling stroked her gently on the head.

"She is so beautiful," the Chinese girl whispered in awe.

Michael took a white leather collar out of his bag. Attached to it was a transmitter about the size of a pack of cigarettes.

"Now we'll be able to keep track of her," he said, clipping the collar around the panda's neck. A small red light on the collar blinked on and off.

"Dr. Tyler, look!" Ling pointed at the creature's chest.

Michael looked down and saw a thin stream of translucent white liquid.

"Either she's pregnant or she's just had a cub," he said, looking around to see if a cub was hiding somewhere close by. As his eyes swept around they caught Ling staring at him, her face filled with excitement.

"Do you know what this means?" she asked eagerly.

Michael nodded slowly, trying not to reveal the excitement he also felt. "Only if it's true and we can prove it," he cautioned her. "Only *then* do we have a chance to keep this reserve open."

3

Ryan and his mother entered the airport terminal. Each of them held one handle of Ryan's dark green duffel bag. They dodged people lugging bags and mothers with screaming kids. Ryan couldn't help thinking about what lay ahead. As usual, his mother was acting fairly neurotic, but it didn't really distract him.

"I sewed name tags in all your underwear," she said as they walked toward the ticket counter.

Ryan could feel his doubts about this whole thing starting to well up uncontrollably. "Mom, I was thinking . . ."

Suddenly his mother stopped in her tracks and shut her eyes.

"What, Mom?" Ryan asked.

"The name tags," she groaned.

"Yeah, that was really nice of you," Ryan said. "I always wanted name tags in my underwear."

"But they're not in Chinese," his mother said. "What good are they?"

She shook her head and started to walk again. Ryan kept up alongside. "Listen, Mom — "

"Remember, Ryan," his mother babbled nervously, "don't eat anything that moves or has eyes. And don't worry, your father will be there. He'll be waiting for you at the gate the *second* you get off the plane."

"I know, Mom, but — "

"If you have any problems, call 911," his mother said.

"In China?" Ryan asked dubiously.

"If they don't have it over there, just tell them you're an American."

They arrived at the ticket counter. Ryan's mom took his plane tickets out of her bag and handed them to the ticket agent behind the counter.

"Window or aisle," the agent said as he typed on a computer.

"Aisle," said Ryan's mom.

"Smoking or non?" the ticket agent asked without looking up.

"He's twelve years old," Mrs. Tyler said.

Ryan realized that they were getting too close for comfort. He had to say something before it was too late. "Mom, this is serious," he began.

"How many bags will you be checking?" the ticket agent asked.

"One," Mrs. Tyler said. But as she started to pick up the duffel bag to put it through the counter, Ryan held the other end and stopped her. His mother looked at him with a puzzled expression.

"Mom, I don't want to go." Ryan felt a small wave of relief. There, he'd said it.

"What?" his mother's eyes widened in astonishment.

"I don't want to go," Ryan said again. "I never wanted to go."

"Why did you wait until now to tell me?" his mother asked, obviously completely bewildered.

Ryan didn't know what to say. He stared down at his feet. Someone behind them cleared his throat. Ryan and his mom both turned. A tall man in a dark suit stood in line, holding two bags.

"I hate to interrupt," the man said, "but some of us *do* want to go."

Mrs. Tyler spun around to the ticket agent. "We'll be right back," she said. Then she led Ryan over to the big picture window that looked out over the runways and airplanes waiting to take off.

"Now, sweetheart," she said in her soothing mommy voice, "I know it must be frightening to go to a strange country on your own."

Ryan shook his head. "I'm not a little kid, Mom. I'm not scared."

"Then what's wrong?" his mother asked him with a frown. "Don't you want to see your father?"

Ryan was quiet for a moment. Then he said, "I'm not sure he really wants to see me."

"Doesn't want to see you?" Mrs. Tyler stared at him in disbelief. "Of course he wants to see you. He sent the tickets, didn't he?"

"Well, yes," Ryan admitted, "but how come in two years I sent him forty-seven letters and he only sent me three?"

Now it was his mother's turn to be quiet for a moment. "Well, hon," she said in a way that made Ryan think she wasn't sure of the answer, "you know how you and Johnny sometimes get when you buy a new Sega game? You get so into it that hours go by and you don't even notice. Well, that's how your father is about his work."

"It hasn't been hours, Mom," Ryan reminded her. "It's been *years*."

"Well, his work is very important to him."

"More important than me?" Ryan asked.

"No, but his work is so big that it blocks out everything else. That doesn't mean that he doesn't love you."

That was bull and Ryan knew it. Three letters in two years was a lousy average.

"Listen, sweetheart," his mother said. "I once heard a saying, 'If you love something, set it free. If it comes back to you, then it's yours forever. If it doesn't, then it never was.' "

That was just more bull as far as Ryan was concerned. "It's been two years," he said. "How much longer do I have to wait for him to come back?"

15

Mrs. Tyler gave him a loving look and patted him on the head. "You know how I know your father loves you?"

Ryan shook his head.

"Because he painted those constellations on your ceiling," his mother said. "And he did it so painstakingly, and it took him so long. Only a father who really loved his son would do such a thing."

A loudspeaker crackled to life nearby, *"Flight 23 to Hong Kong is now boarding through gate 4C."*

"That's your plane," his mother said.

Ryan gave her an uncertain look. Mrs. Tyler reached forward and took the Chicago Cubs baseball cap off his head. Then she smoothed his hair with her hand and started to lead him toward the ticket counter.

"Don't forget," she said, "planes work in both directions. If you don't like it over there you can always come home."

"Promise?" Ryan asked.

"Absolutely," Mrs. Tyler said. Then she put her arms around him and said all the mushy stuff mothers feel compelled to say when their kids go away. Ryan knew he had to go. He couldn't let everyone down.

They went back to the ticket counter and gave the agent the duffel bag. Then Mrs. Tyler walked Ryan down to the gate. "Be sure to brush your teeth every day," she said, "but only with bottled water."

"Sure, Mom." Ryan didn't know if he felt any better about going, but at least getting on the plane would get him away from his mother.

Deep in the forests of the reserve, the female panda busied herself collecting bamboo stalks. Not far away, her cub was chasing a bright blue butterfly. As the cub ran farther and farther away, his mother began to feel alarmed. She let out a short bark and then started after the cub.

Snap! A wire trap snapped closed around her back paw. She pulled at the wire, but that only made the wire cut painfully into her paw. She pulled anyway and called desperately for her cub to come back. But no matter how hard she tried, she couldn't break free.

4

It seemed to Ryan like he traveled forever. The first flight took seventeen hours. The second flight wasn't exactly a short hop either. And unlike the first flight, it wasn't a mixed group of all nationalities. This flight was almost all Chinese people, many of whom gave Ryan funny looks, and none of whom spoke a word of English.

Finally they landed at the Chengdu airport, although to Ryan, calling the place an airport was a stretch. It was more like a couple of big metal Quonset huts stuck together. Military guards wearing green uniforms and carrying rifles stood around, giving him suspicious looks. All the signs were in Chinese. Ryan had no choice but to follow the crowd of passengers inside.

Suddenly a guard in a green uniform grabbed him by the shirt and barked something in Chinese. Ryan didn't have a clue as to what he was saying. The guard said something more and looked pretty annoyed.

Not knowing what else to do, Ryan pulled out his passport. "I'm an American," he said.

The guard turned and called some other official-looking types over. They all wore dark suits and white shirts. They stood around Ryan, looking at him like he came from a different planet. Meanwhile, Ryan looked around, craning his neck for a glimpse of his father.

"I'm looking for my father, Dr. Michael Tyler," he tried to explain.

The men all scowled at him.

"Ty-ler," Ryan said more slowly.

One of the men smiled and nodded. Finally, Ryan thought. Someone who understood! The man pointed toward a door. Ryan took one step, then stopped as the door swung open and a man came out. Through the open doorway, he could see that it was a bathroom. Ryan shook his head slowly. He'd said Tyler, not toilet.

Somehow, without any understanding between himself and anyone else, Ryan managed to collect his duffel bag and make his way out of the air terminal. He stood outside at the curb wondering where in the world his father was while dozens of people rode past on bicycles. Others walked by carrying dead ducks over their shoulders or pushing rickety wooden carts filled with strange-looking vegetables.

Ryan pulled his Cubs cap on. He'd never felt so lost or alone in his whole life. Where was his father? How could he just leave him there?

Then he saw something that gave him hope. A dirty white minivan pulled up to the curb a dozen yards away. On the side was the panda reserve emblem. *It must be his dad!*

Ryan lugged his duffel bag toward the vehicle. Meanwhile, several men in dark suits climbed aboard. The doors started to close! Ryan ran up and banged on them with his fist. A bewildered-looking driver opened the door and stared at him. Ryan looked in and was incredibly disappointed that his father wasn't inside.

"Does this bus go to the panda reserve?" he asked.

The men in dark suits lit cigarettes and stared at Ryan like he was a Martian. Ryan didn't care. He got on the bus and sat down in the back. Wherever they were going, he was going, too.

The headquarters of the reserve was located in a small collection of ramshackle buildings just off the road. There, in one of the shacks, a man named Chang studied a large map on an electronic screen. Here and there on the map were tiny red dots, representing the pandas Michael and his crew had tagged.

Something was bothering Chang, and now he summoned Ling and Michael into the room. Pointing at one of the red dots, he spoke excitedly in Chinese to Ling.

"What's he saying?" Ryan's father asked.

"He said one panda hasn't moved for a long time," Ling answered.

Michael nodded gravely. That could mean any number of things. Unfortunately, none of them were good. He noticed Chang and Ling giving each other looks.

"There's something you're not telling me," Michael said.

Ling said something to Chang, who nodded. Then she turned back to Michael. "It is the mother panda."

Now Michael knew why she'd been reluctant to tell him. If the mother of the cub was hurt or sick, then the cub was in mortal danger. And that meant the whole reserve was in danger. It had been a terrible year for the reserve. Despite their best efforts, they'd been unable to get any of the captive females pregnant. The one cub that had been born in the reserve the year before had died for no apparent reason. And poachers had taken two more cubs from the wild. The panda population in China was severely endangered, but the Chinese government had been threatening to cut off their funding if the reserve couldn't prove it was taking steps to help.

"We have to go to her," Michael said. "Immediately."

5

It wasn't long before Ryan was truly regretting his decision to get on that minivan. They were riding up the side of a mountain on a narrow, winding dirt road. But even calling it a road was a joke. It was more like a sliver of dirt with holes and bumps. Every time the van hit a bump, Ryan bounced up and practically banged his head on the ceiling. Then he'd fall back into his seat again and have the pleasure of looking out the window and straight down about two thousand feet. And forget about guardrails. One wrong move and this minivan was history.

Ryan's stomach felt as if it were up in his throat. The ride was scarier than any roller coaster he'd ever been on. He kept his hands on the seat in front of him, gripping them so tight his knuckles turned white. Forget roller coasters, this was worse than a visit to the dentist!

Ryan spent most of the trip with his eyes closed. If he'd had them open he would have seen that they were gradually climbing into the mountains west of Chengdu, passing some of the most beautiful mountain views in the world. Not only were there vast green forests of evergreens and bamboo, but here and there were broad fields of rhododendron bushes blossoming in vibrant purples, oranges, and yellows. Long pale green-gray streamers of moss hung from the taller spruce trees and black, red, and gold Peking robins hopped among the branches. He might have heard the doglike yaps of the barking deer or caught a glimpse of a rust-colored catlike lynx hunting for rodents.

But all Ryan could think about was getting through this adventure alive. As the minivan bounced along, he wished he'd never listened to his mother. He wished he'd never come.

It wasn't until the minivan stopped climbing that Ryan opened his eyes. They were now on a flattened out stretch of the "road" approaching a tall wooden gate. Beyond the gate was a bunch of rickety-looking buildings. Beside the road was a model of the earth with a mother panda and a little cub sitting on top.

For a moment Ryan forgot to be afraid and was filled with excitement. Could this really be the panda reserve? Had he actually made it here on his own? As the van continued toward the compound, Ryan looked around with eager eyes. Just outside the pagoda-style entrance to the compound, a group of people were busy around an old tractor. The thing looked more like a riding lawnmower. Behind the tractor was a homemade wooden trailer on car tires.

Ryan stared at the people with fascination. One was a skinny, wrinkled old man in tattered clothes drinking some awful-looking brown stuff from a jar. Another Chinese man was eating from a bowl of rice with chopsticks while he gave orders to people. There was a pretty young Chinese girl with long black hair, stowing a backpack in the trailer. And there was — Ryan blinked in astonishment — his father!

Ryan did a double take. His father wasn't exactly what he'd expected. Somehow over the past few years, Ryan's image of Michael had gradually evolved into something like Indiana Jones. The picture Ryan carried in his mind bore only a slight resemblance to the tall, curly haired man with the neatly trimmed, slightly gray beard who he was now staring at.

Ryan's father had been climbing onto the tractor when the minivan arrived. Now he climbed back down. Ryan was eager to greet him, but he had to wait for all the men in the dark suits to get off the van before he could.

"Dad!" he called as he finally got off.

His father continued to come toward him. The Chinese men in the suits were just ahead of Ryan.

"You're early," his father said.

24

"A little," Ryan said. "The plane landed a few minutes . . ." Ryan stopped himself. His father wasn't looking at him or talking to him. He was talking to the men in the suits.

"Yes, Dr. Tyler," one of the men said.

Ryan was shocked. These guys, or at least *one* of them, did speak English after all!

"We are here to make a preliminary report for Mr. Hsu on the progress of the reserve," the man said.

"But we aren't ready for an inspection," Ryan's father said.

"We are only making a preliminary report," the man said. "Mr. Hsu will be here at the end of the week to make the final decision."

"But that's not enough . . ." Ryan's father started to say. Then he stopped and frowned down at Ryan behind the men. "Ryan?"

"Yeah, it's me, Dad." Ryan made his way through the men.

His father stared down at him like he couldn't believe his eyes. "What are you doing here?"

Ryan knew his father could be thick sometimes, but not *that* thick. "You sent me a ticket."

"Your plane's not due until eleven tonight," Michael said.

"Eleven this morning," Ryan corrected him. "You were supposed to meet me."

"This morning?" Michael winced. "Darn, Ryan, I'm sorry. So how'd you get here?"

Ryan pointed back at the minivan.

"Oh, right." Michael nodded. "Good thinking."

Meanwhile the men in the suits were getting impatient. "Dr. Tyler," one said, "I am sorry to interrupt, but we cannot come back. We must inspect now."

Ryan's father turned back to the Chinese officials. "Look, gentlemen, it was my understanding that this reserve was set up to save the panda. And right now I have a panda out there that may be in serious danger, so if you'll excuse me, I have to go." He pointed at one of the men from the reserve. "Chang can answer all your questions."

"Uh, Dad?" Ryan was starting to feel like he'd been forgotten again.

"Right, Ryan," his father said. "Let's get your things into my room."

The pretty Chinese girl picked up Ryan's duffel bag and threw it at him. Ryan caught it and staggered backward. Wow, she had to be pretty strong. He gave her a small smile, but she regarded him coolly.

Slinging the duffel bag over his shoulder, Ryan followed his father through the entrance to the compound. They walked down a central path past the small wooden buildings.

"Well, I'm sorry, Ryan," his father was saying. "It's just bad timing. I've got a situation here I've got to take care of."

Ryan wasn't certain whether he was referring

to the Chinese officials or the panda. They passed a whole group of large cages. Inside, pandas of various sizes climbed around on tree trunks or snoozed. Ryan had never seen a panda this close. They were huge, beautiful, fascinating creatures.

"We'll be back by dark," Michael said, "and then I promise we'll get caught up."

Now Ryan understood. "Why can't I go with you?"

"It's too dangerous out there," his father replied.

In the cages they passed now, the pandas were starting to move toward the bars, as if looking for something. Ryan saw a man coming toward them, pushing a wooden wheelbarrow piled high with green bamboo sticks and leaves. As the worker stopped outside a cage and put a bunch of leaves in, Ryan slowed down and watched the pandas eat.

"You coming?"

Ryan looked up and saw his father standing on the path ahead with his hands on his hips, looking impatient. He hurried to catch up to him.

"How come you keep them in cages?" Ryan asked.

"Because we've been trying to get them to have offspring," his father explained. "Out in the wild there are so few of them that they can't always find each other in the mating season."

Michael led his son into one of the buildings.

Ryan found himself in a small cramped room with a narrow bed and a tiny window. Against one wall was a small wooden desk with an old typewriter. This was his father's room? Not exactly luxury accommodations. His father stood in the doorway, looking preoccupied.

"You must be tired after that trip," Michael said. "Go take a nap or play with the pandas. Just be careful, some of them bite."

Ryan couldn't believe it. He'd come all the way to China just to get blown off by his father? He gave his father an angry look.

"Don't worry, you'll be okay here," Michael said, apparently not noticing. "I'll be back as soon as I can."

Ryan's father turned and left. Ryan was truly peeved. He looked around the room and his eye caught a small, framed photograph. Ryan picked it up. It was a photograph of his father and him on a fishing trip, from years before. Ryan was just a little kid in it, holding a fish that was almost as big as himself. He put the photograph down so hard it almost broke. He felt as if his blood were boiling. After all that time flying, and then that life-threatening ride up that stupid road, he'd come all that way just to have his father say good-bye again. What a jerk!

The sound of an engine caught his attention. Ryan looked out the window and saw his father sitting behind the wheel of the tractor. The pretty girl was sitting on the fender next to him. The girl was wearing a small green day pack. The old Chinese guy was sitting in the trailer behind them.

Darn, Ryan thought. How come it was too dangerous for him to go, but not too dangerous for the old guy and the girl? That was the last straw. Ryan headed out of the room and jogged down the hall. A few moments later he sprinted out through the entrance to the compound. The tractor was already heading off toward the forest, but it was moving so slowly that Ryan was able to catch up to it.

"Dad!" Ryan shouted as he ran. "Hey, Dad! Wait up!"

Without slowing the tractor, Michael looked down at him with a surprised expression.

"Listen, I didn't come all this way to stay in your crummy room and take a nap!" Ryan shouted at him as he ran alongside the tractor.

"Go back," Michael yelled. "It's too dangerous in the forest."

"How come it's too dangerous for me and not for that girl?" Ryan yelled. "She's no tougher than me. If she can do it, I can do it!"

"I don't have time for this right now," his father shouted impatiently. "Just go back to the compound and I *promise* I'll be back soon."

Ryan stopped running and glared at him. "That's what you said two years ago!"

The bitterness of the words must have gotten through his dad's thick skull, because a few moments later Ryan was sitting on the fender next to his father as the tractor slowly climbed upward on a narrow dirt trail through the forest. The old Chinese guy and the young girl now sat behind them on the rickety trailer.

"So how's your mother?" Michael asked.

"She's all right," Ryan said. "I take care of her."

His father gave him a smile. Behind them the girl was speaking harshly in Chinese to the old man. Ryan had no idea what she was saying, but he could tell from her tone that she was angry. He glanced back at her and she just glared at him. Ryan turned to his father.

"Is she mad or something?" he asked.

"Probably," his father replied.

"How come they're here anyway?"

"The old man is Chu," Michael said. "He's been working with pandas all his life. The girl's name is Ling. She's his granddaughter. She works as my translator."

"Translator?" Ryan swallowed, realizing he'd said all sorts of things in front of her. "She speaks English?"

Michael just smiled and nodded.

The route through the forest grew steeper and the trail narrowed even more. The tractor strained and squeaked and struggled up the steep incline. They passed the tree line and started

30

through a broad alpine meadow. Suddenly Ryan heard a loud, metallic *snap!* and the tractor lurched forward.

"What the . . . ?" Michael gasped, twisting around to look behind them. Ryan turned and saw that the trailer had come loose and was careening back down the trail! The old guy, Chu, and the girl were holding on with terrified looks on their faces.

"Come on!" Ryan's father stopped the tractor, then jumped off and started to run back down the hill. Ryan jumped off and followed. Down below the trailer bounced off the trail and wound up with its wheels sinking into a bog. The jolt knocked Chu and Ling off the trailer and onto the ground.

As Ryan and his father got close, Chu and Ling stood up, brushing themselves off and complaining angrily in Chinese. Michael reached them ahead of Ryan.

"Are you all right?" Ryan's father asked.

Bang! Before Ling could answer, a shot rang out in the distance. Everyone spun around and looked up toward the mountains. It was the first time Ryan had really taken in the view, and he was astonished at how high and beautiful the peaks were.

"What was that?" he asked.

Chu said something in Chinese.

"Huh?" Ryan said.

"Give me the blowgun," Michael said, reaching for a long, thin tube tied to the side of the trailer.

"But it might be dangerous," Ling cautioned him in English.

"Dad, what's she talking about?" Ryan asked.

"Poachers," his father said, sliding the blowgun over his shoulder and taking some kind of electronic device out of the trailer. The thing was about the size of a shoe box with a hoop-shaped antenna sticking out of it.

Chu said something else in Chinese.

"He says it is too dangerous," Ling interpreted.

"I'll be all right," Ryan's father said. "You guys stay here."

The next thing Ryan knew, his father disappeared into the thick green underbrush, leaving him with Chu and Ling.

6

Farther up the mountain, two leathery-skinned poachers moved slowly through the underbrush. They both wore tattered clothes and sandals. The older man, Shong, carried an old rusty hunting rifle on his shoulder. He was followed by a younger man named Po.

Soon they came to the clearing where the mother panda sat, still trapped by the wire around her paw. Her cub sat next to her. As the poachers stepped into the clearing, she reared back apprehensively. But it had been a long time since she had eaten and her strength was ebbing.

Shong turned to Po and spoke in Chinese, "She is too weak to fight. Take the cub from her."

Po stepped toward the cub, who instinctively backed toward his mother and clung to her fur. Po grabbed the cub and pulled him away. His mother made a halfhearted effort to grab the cub back, but she was tired and the trap stopped her. The wire had already cut deeply into her paw and every movement now caused a great surge of pain. Po put the frightened cub in a rope basket and walked back to Shong.

The older poacher raised his rifle and aimed it at the mother panda.

"Her pelt will bring us lots of money," he said in Chinese.

"Look." Po pointed at the white leather collar around her neck. "The collar."

The small red light on the collar was flashing quickly, as if alert to the fact that Michael was nearby and coming closer. Po sensed that trouble was on the way. He put his hand on Shong's shoulder.

"Let's go," he said. "The cub's enough."

"No." Shong shook Po's hand off and aimed the rifle again at the giant panda.

He had just started to pull the trigger when Michael burst through the underbrush, shouting. As Shong swung around, Ryan's father tried to grab the gun. Both men rolled to the ground, wrestling for the rifle.

Bang! A shot rang out!

Michael felt a bolt of searing hot pain shoot through his left leg just above the knee. He'd been shot! Grimacing in agony, he let go of Shong and grabbed his leg.

Po pulled Shong up and spoke urgently in Chinese. Shong grunted something in agreement, and the two poachers hurried away into the underbrush with the cub.

Down below, Ryan and the others had heard the second gunshot. Ling had instantly cried out Michael's name and rushed into the undergrowth. The old man, Chu, ran after her. Suddenly Ryan realized they'd left him alone. The next decision was an easy one. He hurried after them.

Ling must've been pretty fast, and for an old guy Chu could sure cover the rough ground quickly. Ryan had to sweep brush, vines, and branches out of the way as he pushed forward. By the time he reached the clearing, he found the girl and old man kneeling beside his father. Michael was sitting up with his back against a tree. The thigh of his left pant leg was blood red. Across the clearing sat a large panda.

Ryan didn't have time to ask what it was doing there. He couldn't take his eyes off his father's wound.

"Dr. Tyler!" Ling cried. "Are you all right?"

But his father wasn't even thinking about the wound anymore. "There were two of them. They took the cub."

Ryan couldn't believe it. His father had just gotten shot and all he could talk about was some panda cub.

The old guy said something to Ling in Chinese. She removed a bandanna from her neck and handed it to him. Chu tied it around Michael's leg to stop the bleeding.

"I am worried about you," Ling said to Michael. Ryan could see that she was truly concerned for his father.

"Don't worry," Ryan's father replied. "It's only a flesh wound."

Chu barked some kind of order at Ling, who nodded and turned to Michael.

"I'll go back to the trailer to radio for a helicopter," Ling said, and started back through the underbrush.

Ryan heard a scraping sound and turned to see that Chu had gone over to the panda and was trying to cut some kind of wire that held one of her back paws. Ryan looked back questioningly at his father.

"We have to save her for the cub's sake," Michael explained.

Ryan nodded slowly. He still couldn't get over the fact that his father seemed more concerned for the pandas than for himself.

Whump-uh-whump-uh-whump-uh . . . It wasn't long before Ryan heard the chopping sound of a distant helicopter approaching. Looking up at the sky above the clearing, he saw a small helicopter appear and start to descend toward them.

The branches of the trees at the edge of the clearing began to shake, and loose leaves began to whirl around as the chopper came closer. The underbrush shook wildly and bits of grass and dust flew into the air. The sound of the engines grew into a roar as Ryan and the others shielded their eyes from the blowing debris.

A moment later the helicopter landed and a Chinese pilot hopped out. He and Chu started to help the weakened panda into the helicopter. It was becoming obvious to Ryan that in this part of the world, pandas came first. Still sitting with his back against the tree, Michael issued commands.

"Gently!" he yelled as the men strained to lift the large panda into the helicopter. "Easy with her. Take that collar off! It'll help her breathe a little easier."

Ling ran over and took the white leather collar off the panda. She put it in her day pack. Once they had the panda in the helicopter, Chu and the pilot turned their attention to Ryan's father. Michael groaned as they helped him up and supported him as he walked toward the helicopter.

Michael turned to his son. "Ryan, you sit up front."

Ryan had never flown in a helicopter before. As he started toward the front, the pilot raised his hand. "No. Too much weight already."

Ryan looked back at his father.

"What's wrong?" Michael asked.

"Too much weight for the helicopter," the pilot said. "There's no room for the boy."

"Then take him back and I'll wait here," Ryan's father said.

That didn't make any sense. The reason they'd called for the helicopter was to help Ryan's father.

"I'll drop you and the panda off," the pilot said to Michael. "Then I'll come back."

"No." Michael shook his head. "Ryan can't stay here."

Ryan was worried about his father's wound. He was worried about how much blood he'd lost. "I can stay here."

"We must hurry," the pilot said. "I need to come back before dark."

Michael thought for a moment, then turned toward his son. "Okay, I'll let you stay, but you have to stay right here. Promise me you won't move from this spot."

"Hey, don't worry," Ryan assured him. He wasn't going anywhere.

"He'll be right back to pick you up," his father said.

Ryan could see that his father wasn't happy about leaving him behind. In a way it made him feel a little better. At least his father seemed to care. The pilot slid the door closed and Ryan watched him climb in front. A few moments later the helicopter blades began to turn. Ryan and the others ducked and covered their eyes as things began to fly around again. Then the helicopter lifted off and rose into the sky.

Ryan watched it disappear behind the trees. Then he turned and looked around. He could see nothing but thick green forest and underbrush in every direction. He'd just been left somewhere in the middle of western China with a girl who didn't like him and an old man he couldn't understand.

7

Ryan sat with his back against a tree. Ling sat across the clearing, purposely not looking at him. In the middle of the clearing the old guy, Chu, was on his hands and knees with his face practically touching the ground. If Ryan hadn't known better, he would have thought the guy was looking for a contact lens.

Ryan turned to Ling. "What's he doing?"

Ling ignored him.

Suddenly Chu jumped to his feet, looking excited and jabbering away in Chinese. Ling rose to her feet and chattered excitedly, too. Chu started waving arms around. Ling stood with her hands on her hips, shaking her head and arguing with him.

"Would someone please tell me what's going on?" Ryan asked.

They both ignored him, talking and arguing excitedly. Then, without warning, Chu ran off into the undergrowth.

"Hey!" Ryan gasped nervously, "where's he going?"

"He's right," Ling said.

"Right about what?" Ryan asked.

"We must bring the cub back to the reserve," Ling said, pulling her day pack on. "Without its mother's milk it will die."

Ling started toward the edge of the clearing where Chu had just disappeared.

"Wait a minute!" Ryan cried. "You can't just leave me."

Ling paused and thought for a second. "Then come."

"Are you crazy?" Ryan asked. "I can't. I'm not risking my life for some panda. Besides, you heard my father. He said I was supposed to wait here."

"Okay, wait," Ling said. "Make yourself happy."

The Chinese girl turned and headed off into the underbrush.

"Fine, go!" Ryan shouted after her. "Who needs you? I earned a couple of merit badges in the Boy Scouts. I know how to take care of myself in the wild!"

Ling didn't answer. Ryan could no longer see her. Suddenly he was alone. The forest around the clearing was quiet. Ryan looked up into the air, waiting hopefully for the helicopter to return. But the only thing above him in the sky were a couple of bugs. Then one of the trees at the edge of the clearing began to shake. Ryan gasped and jumped back, his heart pounding in his chest.

The tree shook again and Ryan realized it was just a monkey. Ryan breathed a slight sigh of relief, but he still felt scared. His father had told him to wait there, he reminded himself. His father had said he'd be safe.

Safe?

He was alone on the side of a mountain somewhere in the middle of nowhere. He didn't know where he was. No one spoke English and there were no phones to call 911. There were monkeys and big panda bears and who knew what else sneaking around in the woods. He pulled off his Cubs cap and slid his fingers through his hair, then pulled the cap back on.

Then Ryan felt a horrible sensation. Something heavy and cold was slithering over his feet. Ryan looked down. It was a snake!

"Ahhhhh!" The next thing he knew, air was emptying out of his lungs in a scream. He was running through the underbrush in the direction Ling had gone, shouting, "Hey, Ling! Wait for me!"

He had to fight his way through the thick underbrush, knocking branches and vines out of the way with wild swipes of his arms.

"Ling!" he yelled. "Chu!"

No answer.

"Come on, guys," he called. "You couldn't

have gone that far! Where'd you guys go . . .
owhooooa!"

Thunk! Ryan tripped over a fallen tree trunk
and fell forward to the ground. With his chin on
the soft soil, he stared ahead where the plants
grew out of the dirt. A patch of young bamboo
shoots had sprung up nearby. As Ryan stared at
them, one of them began to wiggle mysteriously.

What in the world? Ryan thought.

Suddenly the wiggling shoot was yanked downward into the ground and disappeared!

Ryan jumped to his feet. Now what? How did
that happen? He didn't have a clue. All he knew
was that things had just gone from bad to worse.
He was alone. Utterly and totally alone in a weird
country where weird stuff was happening.

Then he heard something. It sounded like hu-
man voices. He stayed still and listened. There
they were again . . . voices . . . Chinese voices
coming through the underbrush.

Ryan started to follow the voices. He doubted
it was Chu and Ling, but even if it was some
villagers, maybe they could help him find his way
back to the panda reserve.

Soon he came to a clearing. Ahead of him, a
narrow rope bridge led across a deep ravine. Ryan
could hear the sound of water rushing below
and knew there must have been a river running
through the ravine.

The bridge was made of rope and wooden slats.

It looked awfully rickety. Two men in tattered clothes were just starting to cross the bridge. One of them was carrying a basket on his back.

Still standing in the undergrowth, Ryan stuck his fingers in his mouth and whistled as loudly as he could. The men on the bridge turned and looked around.

"Hey!" Ryan shouted and waved. "Over he — "

A leathery hand clamped down on his mouth, and Ryan felt himself being dragged back into the underbrush. Ryan struggled and turned to face his assailant. It was Chu!

The old Chinese man started to talk to him in a hushed, urgent voice. Up close his breath stank and his teeth were rotten. Ling was standing next to him. Ryan turned to her.

"What'd he say?" he asked.

"Shut up."

"Oh." Ryan frowned. "Why?"

Ling pointed at the men on the rope bridge. "Poachers."

The old man stuck his finger in his mouth, then held it up in the air. Then he pulled the glass jar out of his pocket and took a drink. When he finished, he screwed the top back on the jar and motioned them to follow him.

They waited at the edge of the underbrush until the poachers were across the bridge. Then Chu started out. Ryan suddenly realized the old man was going to cross the bridge. He looked back quizzically at Ling behind him, but she simply regarded him with a blank gaze.

Then she headed for the bridge.

Ryan got up and followed. They reached the bridge. Chu had already started across it without breaking stride. Ryan stopped and looked down. Just as he'd guessed, a churning river rushed through the ravine below. Ryan placed one foot on the first wooden plank and felt it sink under his weight. The rope was gray and weather-beaten. The bridge swayed loosely. Ryan couldn't believe it would support his weight. He stopped and looked back at Ling who was now behind him.

"Maybe we should wait for the helicopter to come back," he said nervously.

"By then it may be too late," Ling replied. "Go."

Ryan hesitated. "Look at this thing! It's ancient."

Ling shook her head. "It's safe. See grandfather."

Ryan looked across the bridge to the other side, where Chu was waving at them impatiently.

"Go," Ling said again.

Ryan stepped out a few feet and then froze. The bridge swung back and forth and the water rushed past below.

"Don't look down," Ling said behind him.

"It's a little too late for that," Ryan groaned.

Meanwhile, Chu was shouting and gesturing on the other side of the bridge.

"What's he saying?" Ryan asked.

"I can't hear," Ling said. "The water is too loud. Now hurry! The panda cub is in trouble!"

But Ryan shook his head and started to turn around. "Sorry, but there's no way I'm crossing this bridge. It's — "

He stopped talking. Now that he'd turned around, he could see that something was behind Ling. He didn't know what it was, only that it was big, brown, furry, and sort of looked like a cross between a giant goat and an ox with pointed curved horns. And whatever it was, it had lowered its head and was scraping at the ground with its hooves as if it was preparing to charge.

"*Ahhhhhh!*" Ryan heard himself scream.

8

Ling spun around, saw the thing, then started onto the bridge toward Ryan. "Run!"

"What is it?" Ryan gasped.

"Takin," Ling said. "It's not friendly."

"Yeah, I could have guessed that." Ryan started to run across the bridge. Ling was right behind him. Some of the wooden slats fell out of the bridge as they ran.

Somehow Ryan made it to the other side without falling through the slats and plummeting down to the raging river below. He quickly turned and looked back at the hairy takin. The beast had followed them partway across the bridge and then stopped because the slats had fallen and it couldn't go any farther.

"He almost killed us," Ryan gasped, breathing hard from the dash across the bridge.

The old Chinese guy, Chu, started to laugh.

"What's so funny?" Ryan asked.

Chu said something in Chinese.

"Grandfather thought you were very funny," Ling translated.

"Glad *he's* having fun," Ryan muttered.

Chu said something else in Chinese and started into the woods on the other side of the ravine. Ryan and Ling followed. Soon they came to a rocky area. The old Chinese man stopped, licked his finger, and held it up in the air. Ryan had seen him do this enough times to really start wondering about it.

"Is there like radar in his finger?" he asked Ling.

"Grandfather is very wise," Ling replied.

That may have been true, but Ryan sort of winced at the thought of what that finger must've tasted like.

Chu said something in Chinese and pointed. Ryan saw a thin tendril of smoke rising just over a nearby ridge. Chu gestured for them to move closer to the ridge. They pressed themselves against some rocks and peeked over. Down below Ryan saw the dark opening of a cave. The smoke was coming from a small fire at its mouth.

Again, Chu spoke in Chinese.

"What'd he say?" Ryan whispered.

"This is the poachers' cave," Ling whispered back.

If that was the poachers' cave, then Ryan knew he was as close as he wanted to be.

48

"Great," he whispered to Ling. "Now that we know where they live, why can't we go back, report 'em to the panda police, and let them take over?"

"It's not so easy," Ling whispered back.

Chu backed away from the ridge and motioned them to follow him to a nearby stand of trees. There he stood and stared at one tree, rubbing his hand against his chin. Ryan and Ling sat nearby and watched.

"What's he doing?" Ryan asked.

"He's thinking of a plan to rescue the cub," Ling said.

That sounded good, but Ryan had his doubts. The old guy didn't seem so smart to him. Maybe he was just staring at the tree and didn't have a clue as to how to save the cub.

Whomp-uh-whomp-uh-whomp-uh. . . . The distant sound of a helicopter brought Ryan to his feet. He could hear it, but he couldn't see it. He ran up on the ridge to get a better look. There it was, way out over the valley, flying slowly toward them.

"Hey!" Ryan shouted and waved his arms. "Here! Over here!"

He was only barely aware that Ling and Chu were also waving, not at the helicopter, but at him. Ryan ignored them and kept waving and shouting at the helicopter.

Now Ling and Chu came running toward him.

"Be quiet!" Ling hissed. "Keep your voice down."

Ryan pointed excitedly at the helicopter. "We gotta make sure they see us."

"No, stop!" Ling said. "The poachers will see us."

But Ryan kept shouting and waving. He didn't care about the poachers. He just wanted to get out of there and —

Wham! Ling punched him as hard as she could in the nose. Ryan's eyes rolled up into his head and he slumped to the ground, unconscious.

Night was falling. The hospital in the panda reserve was nothing more than a dimly lit room with a large wooden bench that served as an operating table, and a cabinet with some crude medical supplies. The female panda lay on the bench under anesthesia. Her half-open eyes were glazed. Chang had given her the name Chih while they were in the helicopter. He now stood over her, gently sewing the deep wounds on her paw from the wire trap. Michael stood beside him. His leg was bandaged and he needed a wooden cane for support.

"Hang in there, Chih," he said under his breath. "You're doing great."

Through the open window came the distant

sound of the helicopter returning. Michael quickly turned and limped toward the door, leaning on the cane.

Outside the helicopter landed and Lei, the pilot, got out. Michael felt a jolt of surprise. There was no sign of Ryan and the others.

"Where are they?" he asked the pilot.

"I'm so sorry." Lei shook his head slowly. "I cannot find them and the boy."

Michael didn't understand. He'd given Ryan strict orders not to leave the spot. "What do you mean, you can't find them? Didn't you go back to the spot?"

"I went to the spot," Lei said. "I circled many times, but I did not see them."

"They had to be there," Michael said. He simply couldn't believe that they would have left. Not Ryan.

"Maybe they built camp for the night," Lei said. "They got tired and decided to sleep in the forest."

The explanation didn't matter to Michael. The only thing that mattered was finding his son. "We have to go back," he said.

"No, it is night," Lei said. "We can't fly in the dark. We'll go back in the morning."

Michael knew Lei was right. Trying to fly a helicopter through the mountains at night was suicide. He just couldn't understand why Ryan hadn't been there.

"I told him to wait," he said in frustration.

"Don't worry," Lei said. "The boy is safe with Chu and Ling."

Michael just stared out toward the mountains. He wanted to believe that it was true. But the truth was, he wasn't so sure.

9

Ryan opened his eyes. He was lying on some sort of mat in a little cabin with stone walls. Sunlight streamed through the windows and it felt like morning. His nose throbbed painfully. He carefully prodded it with his fingers. It felt swollen, but not broken. Wow, that Ling sure could punch.

Ryan pushed himself to his feet. The cabin was empty except for a broken chair and a small, dusty table. He saw now that there were no windows, just open squares in the stone walls to let in light.

Ryan walked out through the space where a door had once been. Outside the sun was bright and he had to shield his eyes from the glare. The sky was blue and the leaves on the trees shimmered. A small, sparkling stream rippled down through the woods past the cabin.

Chu was standing near the stream, making strange, karatelike movements in slow motion. It sort of looked like a dance, or someone pretending to fight an invisible enemy. Ryan had watched enough TV shows to know that it was called *tai chi*.

But seeing it in person was sort of amazing, and for an old guy, Chu moved with remarkable grace. Without completely realizing it, Ryan began to copy Chu's movements. Just as Chu spun around on one foot, so did Ryan . . . to find Ling standing behind him with a smile on her face.

Ryan quickly pretended to stretch and yawn. "So, uh, what's up?"

Ling reached toward him and he jumped back.

"You're not gonna hit me again, are you?" Ryan asked nervously.

"It depends if you do something stupid or not," Ling replied.

"Yeah, well, you sucker-punched me anyway," Ryan said. "I never had a chance."

Once again, Ling reached toward him. Ryan looked down and saw something brown and wrinkled in her hand.

"What is it?" he asked.

"Breakfast," Ling said.

Ryan took it and smelled it. Then he bit off a little piece and chewed it. Now he knew what it was.

"This is beef jerky, not breakfast," he said. "Breakfast is blueberry pancakes with maple syrup, bacon on the side, and two eggs over easy."

Ling just frowned at him. Ryan pointed at the

dried meat. "This is a treat you give your dog when he rolls over."

"So roll over, then eat it," Ling said with a shrug.

Ryan took another nibble. He couldn't believe he was going to eat this thing. It tasted more like his baseball mitt than food. But he was hungry.

Chu came over and spoke to Ling in Chinese. Then he pointed at Ryan and said something.

"What'd he say?" Ryan asked Ling.

"Grandfather says since you practiced *tai chi*, you are now a warrior ready to battle the poachers," Ling answered with a smirk.

"Is he serious?" Ryan asked nervously.

Ling just smiled at him. Chu said something more in Chinese. Ling turned to Ryan and translated. "He says the poachers have gone so we should go to the cave."

Going to the cave was the last thing Ryan wanted to do, but he couldn't say so. Between getting punched in the nose and being made fun of because of the *tai chi*, his ego had been bruised enough for one day. Once again they climbed up on the ridge and peeked at the poachers' cave. One of the poachers was sitting at the opening of the cave with his arms crossed and his head bowed, asleep.

"I thought you said they were gone," Ryan whispered.

"They must have come back," Ling said.

Chu whispered something in Chinese and then began to move away.

"He's leaving us?" Ryan gasped, alarmed.

"He'll watch for the other poacher," Ling said in a low voice. "If he sees him, Grandfather will whistle to warn us. Come, we must get closer."

Ling got up and started to scamper over the rock ridge closer to the cave. Ryan looked around and realized he had no choice but to follow. As they crept closer to the cave, Ling accidentally dislodged a rock with her foot. The rock began to fall, clunking into other rocks and causing a small rock slide.

Ling and Ryan quickly ducked down as the noise woke the poacher. Instantly alert, the poacher quickly looked around. Then he got up and went into the cave.

"What if he's going to get his buddy?" Ryan asked. A moment later the poacher returned with his rifle. Once again he looked around. Seeing no one, he settled back down at the entrance to the cave, keeping the rifle within arm's reach. Ryan figured that ended any possible assault on the cave, but Ling still hadn't moved.

"Hey, come on," he whispered. "How do you expect us to take him when he's got a rifle?"

Ling reached into the day pack she was carrying and pulled out a long hollow tube. Ryan knew it was a blowgun. She couldn't be serious. What chance did a girl with a blowgun stand against a man with a rifle?

But Ling started to crawl closer and Ryan followed. Soon they were only a dozen yards away. Ling raised the blowgun and tried to aim it at the poacher, who'd started to doze again. But a rock blocked her angle.

"Maybe we should just go," Ryan whispered.

"Shh . . ." Ling seemed annoyed.

"Listen," Ryan said in a low voice. "That guy has a gun with *real* bullets. What are you gonna do with that blowgun? Hit him with a spitball?"

Ling leveled her gaze on him. "You are nothing like your father. Dr. Tyler is brave."

Ryan winced. The words stung. Meanwhile, Ling was still trying to get a good angle on the poacher. Finally she lowered the blowgun and shook her head.

"The angle is no good," she said. "He needs to be more to the left."

Still smarting from the insult Ling just delivered, Ryan decided to show her just how brave he could be. She needed a better angle for her blowgun? Okay, he'd give it to her. He jumped out from behind the rock and faced the poacher. He pulled off his Cubs cap and waved it.

"Hey, you stupid poacher!" he yelled. "Over here, dorkbrain!"

The poacher looked up startled.

"Yo, genius, that's right," Ryan called, hoping Ling now had the angle she needed.

The poacher lifted his rifle and aimed it at Ryan, who couldn't understand why Ling hadn't shot him yet. It suddenly occurred to Ryan that maybe she wasn't going to.

"*Ahhhhh!*" Ryan tossed his cap in the air, then turned and ran toward the forest. He kept waiting to hear the blast of the rifle, but nothing happened. Finally, he slowed and looked back. The poacher was still standing there. Suddenly the rifle dropped out of his hands. Then the poacher himself keeled over and hit the ground.

Ryan started back toward the cave. Up ahead, Ling walked up to the fallen poacher and kicked the rifle away with her foot. Ryan joined her. Ling gave him a curious look.

"You're crazy." But she smiled as she said it.

"Hey, you needed a better angle, right?" Ryan replied proudly.

Ling nodded and stepped into the dark cave. Ryan didn't particularly like caves, but it looked as if he was going to follow her anyway. He went inside. The cave was lit here and there with crude, handmade torches. The walls were lined with rocks.

"Looks like we've got the wrong cave," Ryan said. "I don't see any cubs in here."

Ling went around a bend in the cave and stopped, then rushed ahead. Ryan turned the corner and found her sorting through a pile of animal hides. When she came across two black-and-white panda hides, her face twisted as if she wanted to scream with anger and cry at the same time. Ryan picked up one of the hides and ran his hand over it. The fur was surprisingly coarse and stiff, not at all like the soft fur he'd expected to feel.

"Why do they want these?" he asked, holding up the panda hide.

"To sell," Ling said. Her voice filled with disgust and her eyes started to glisten with tears.

"You think one of these is the cub?" Ryan asked.

Ling shook her head. "They'll keep the cub alive to sell it to a zoo."

Suddenly she saw something and quickly stepped over to it. It was the rope basket the poachers had been carrying. Something inside was making scratching noises. It must be the cub! The lid of the basket was tied shut with rope. Ling was trying to undo the knot, but she wasn't having much success.

"Here, let me," Ryan said. "I can get it."

Ling backed away from the basket and let Ryan try. Unfortunately, the knot was as tight as a rock and he couldn't get it loose either.

"You made it worse," Ling said accusingly.

"Did not," Ryan said. "It's just tighter than I thought. Go check Sleeping Beauty. See if he's got a knife on him."

* * *

Ling left the cave and kneeled down next to the unconscious poacher. She pulled the dart out of his hip, then searched his pockets, but they were empty.

Ryan called to her from inside the cave. "Hurry up. I don't want to be here when his friend comes back."

Ling rolled her eyes. Neither did she. The boy was nothing like his father, who she admired greatly. The father only cared about saving pandas. The boy only cared about himself.

Ling rolled the poacher over, hoping to check any pockets she hadn't gotten to yet. Suddenly she felt something poke her in the back. It was hard and round and made out of metal. She didn't have to turn around to know it was the barrel of the rifle.

10

Inside the cave, Ryan was finally able to get the knot on the basket loosened. He was just about to open the lid when the whole basket fell over and something black and white tumbled out. It was the cub. It sat up and blinked at him with its little black eyes.

Ryan had to smile to himself. Rarely in his life had he seen anything so adorable. It was the size of a large teddy bear and probably weighed about twenty pounds. But it had the gentle harmlessness of a little kitten.

"So you're what all the fuss is about," Ryan said.

Now Ling and Chu came into the cave and joined him. Ling looked pale and shaken.

"What happened to you?" Ryan asked.

"Grandfather played a trick," she said, giving Chu an annoyed look. "He poked a rifle at me."

Chu, meanwhile, picked the panda cub up and studied it closely. He uttered something in Chinese.

"Grandfather says the cub needs milk," Ling said. "We must bring it back to its mother quickly."

"What about these hides?" Ryan asked. "We'll need 'em to nail those guys."

"Nail?" Ling frowned.

"Like to get 'em busted," Ryan explained.

"Busted?"

"Arrested," Ryan said. "These hides prove that they're poachers."

"No, it's too much to carry," Ling said. "It'll slow us down. We can only take the cub. We must go fast."

Chu said something in Chinese, pointing at the poacher who lay on the ground at the entrance to the cave. Ryan got the feeling it had something to do with getting out of there before the guy woke up.

They headed out of the cave, stepping over the poacher. As Ling stepped over him, she paused. Then, to Ryan's astonishment, she reared back and kicked the man as hard as she could. Ryan was stunned by her passion and anger. These people really cared about pandas.

They started back down the side of the mountain, working their way through the forest. Ryan was amazed that the old man seemed to know the way back. But it was slow going. The forest was very dense and they used a great deal of energy pushing vines and branches out of the way.

After a while, Chu put the cub on the ground and sat on a rock. He shook his head and said something to Ling in Chinese. Ryan could tell he was tired.

"We'll rest for a while," Ling said.

They sat and watched the cub crawl around. Ryan reached up to pull his baseball cap off, and suddenly realized he wasn't wearing it. He must've left it back at the poachers' cave. Darn, he really liked that cap.

Meanwhile, the cub watched a thin shoot of baby bamboo wiggle mysteriously and then vanish into the ground.

"Hey!" Ryan said, remembering seeing that before. "What's that?"

"What?" Ling asked, looking in his direction.

Another shoot of bamboo had begun to wiggle and Ryan pointed at it. "That."

This time the panda cub jumped forward, playfully trying to grab the shoot, but it disappeared before the baby panda could get its paws on it.

Ling laughed.

"That's a bamboo rat," she explained. "It makes a tunnel underground to steal bamboo."

Now another shoot began to wiggle. The panda cub leaped at it, but it disappeared. The little cub looked around in astonishment. Ryan and Ling both laughed.

Chu pulled out his jar with the brown liquid in it. He took a gulp, then belched and held the jar out to Ryan.

Ryan shook his head. "Thanks, but I'll pass."

But Chu pushed the jar into his hands, uttering something in Chinese. Ryan glanced dismally at Ling.

"Grandfather says you have to drink something," she translated. "He will be insulted if you do not share a drink with him."

Ryan sighed and looked down at the brownish liquid, trying not to imagine what it was made of. He felt a little ill inside, but mustered his courage and took a sip. *It was awful!* Ryan made a face. The stuff was bitter and tasted like stagnant water mixed with soy sauce.

"That was truly gross," he said, quickly handing the jar back.

Chu smiled and said something to his granddaughter.

"Grandfather says it is good for you," Ling interpreted. "It will grow hair between your toes."

"Just what I always wanted," Ryan muttered, rolling his eyes.

Chu said something more with a big grin. To Ryan's surprise, Ling blushed and shook her head. Chu nudged her, urging her to translate.

"Grandfather said some women like hair between the toes," Ling said uncomfortably, not meeting Ryan's gaze.

Ryan had to smile. Chu gave him a big wink. The old guy was okay.

The younger poacher, Po, returned to the cave carrying two rabbits he'd shot. He found Shong sprawled on the ground by the entrance. At first he thought Shong must have fallen asleep, but then he saw the open basket. The panda cub was gone!

"Shong!" Po shook his friend's shoulder.

Shong slowly opened his eyes. He looked very groggy.

"What happened?" Po asked in Chinese. "Where's the cub?"

Shong thought back to the last thing he'd seen, and told Po about the Western boy who'd come running out from the rocks, taunting him.

"A boy?" Po asked.

Shong nodded and held out his hand, indicating Ryan's height.

Po nodded grimly. That cub was worth more than all their pelts combined. They had to get it back.

"We'll find him," Po said. "He can't have gone very far."

Shong stood up and brushed himself off. Then he noticed Ryan's Chicago Cubs cap lying on the ground. He picked it up and studied it carefully, a thought forming in his mind.

11

They'd started moving again. Chu led the way. Ryan came second and Ling, now carrying the cub, brought up the rear. The forest was so dense they could barely see the sky through the thick canopy of leaves above.

But they could hear. *Whump-uh-whump-uh-whump . . .*

"It's the helicopter!" Ryan shouted. "Come on, we gotta get out in the open so he'll see us!"

Ryan started to run through the trees, searching for an open place, but the dense thatch above seemed to go on forever. An awful thought struck him. *They were never going to see him down here!*

He looked around desperately for a place where the sunlight came through, but there was none to be found. Just tree trunks for as far as he could see in every direction.

Whump-uh-whump . . . whum . . . the sound of the helicopter was fading. Ryan felt his heart sink. It was leaving. At this rate they were never going to get saved.

He walked slowly back to the others, half expecting Chu to grin knowingly or laugh at him. But the old man looked as grim as Ryan felt. He jerked his head and they started to walk again.

They became spread out as they walked. Now Ryan was in the rear. He could just see Ling through the underbrush. Chu was too far ahead to see.

A little while later, Ling stopped at the edge of a clearing. Ryan stopped beside her. He could hear the sound of rushing water. Ahead was the flimsy footbridge that stretched across the ravine.

"Not this again," Ryan mumbled.

Ling looked back at him. "Is the American boy afraid?"

"No," Ryan said defensively. "I'm just worried about Chu. He might get hurt being an old man and all."

Just then they heard a shout. Looking across the ravine, they saw Chu waving. The old man had already crossed the bridge!

Now Ling started across the bridge. "Come on, we must cross the bridge and get back to the radio."

Ryan watched her walk across, stepping over the open spaces where the slats had fallen away during their last trip. He took a deep breath and placed one foot on the bridge, holding onto the ropes that served as a handrail.

Don't look down, he told himself. Look anywhere you want, but not down.

He got a little way across the bridge and began to feel better. This wasn't so bad after all. In fact, he'd show Ling he wasn't scared. He stopped on the bridge and let go of the ropes, raising his hands in the air.

"Hey, Ling!" he shouted. "Look! No hands!"

Ling had just crossed the halfway point of the bridge. She turned to look at him, but her reaction was not what he expected. She pointed and screamed!

Ryan twisted around and looked back. The two poachers were standing at the edge of the clearing, aiming their guns at him!

High above the reserve in the helicopter, Michael felt a dismal sensation in the pit of his stomach as he stared down at the thick green forest below. Ryan, Ling, and Chu could be anywhere down there. They could have been directly under the helicopter and he wouldn't have known it.

Lei, the pilot, gave him a questioning look.

"Let's go find the equipment," Michael said. "Maybe they went back there."

Lei nodded and steered the chopper back toward the clearing where Michael had instructed Ryan to wait for them. The helicopter settled down in a small cloud of dust and leaves. Lei and Chang got out. Michael followed slowly, wincing in pain as he limped on the cane.

Up ahead, he saw that Lei and Chang had stopped by the trailer. His son and the others weren't there. Michael swore silently to himself. Where were they?

Lei must have read the worry in his face. "We'll look in this area. They cannot be too far away."

Michael nodded and turned to Chang, who was trying to pick up a signal from the white leather collar with the tracking antenna.

"You picking anything up?" Ryan's father asked. He was certain he'd seen Ling put the collar in her day pack.

"Nothing," Chang said. "The collar is not activated."

"It's not sending out any signals," Lei said.

Michael sighed and shook his head in frustration. They should have gotten a signal from the collar, no matter where it was. Why they weren't getting it was just another mystery.

Bang! At the sound of the gunshot, the three men straightened up. Michael pointed to the west.

"It came from over there!" he yelled. Chang and Lei took off through the forest. Michael followed, as fast as his cane and bad leg would allow.

The shot had missed Ryan, but it came so close that he actually heard the bullet whiz past him. He stood on the bridge in frozen disbelief. He thought the poacher would fire again, but the second poacher stopped him.

Ryan spun around, determined to get off the bridge before the poachers changed their minds and started shooting again. A dozen yards in front of him, Ling also turned to run, but her foot missed a slat and she started to fall through the bridge!

"Ling!" Ryan shouted. He watched in horror as the cub fell out of her arms and tumbled onto the bridge. Ling fell through the slats, but managed to grab one of the ropes. The next thing he knew, she was hanging there with the wild, turbulent waters rushing beneath her.

Ryan raced quickly toward her, stepping carefully to make sure he didn't fall, too. When he reached the slats nearest her, he kneeled down to help.

Bang! Another shot rang out! Ryan ducked, then realized the bullet hadn't been meant for him. The poachers were aiming at Chu, who had started across the clearing toward the bridge when he saw Ling fall through.

Now Chu dove for cover behind a rock. The

poachers were running across the clearing toward the bridge. Ryan knew they wanted the cub.

Ling shouted something in Chinese. Ryan reached down toward her.

"Grab my hand!" he yelled. As he struggled to reach her, a few more slats fell out of the bridge and into the rushing white water below.

Ling grabbed his hand. Ryan held on tight and tried to pull her up. Suddenly something heavy pounced on his back!

"Hey!" Ryan shouted and twisted around. It was the panda cub, now clinging to his back.

"Don't let go!" Ling screamed below him. "I can't swim!"

"I won't!" Ryan shouted back. But the slats kept falling away. Ryan didn't know how much longer the remaining slats could hold his weight.

Crack! He soon found out. The remaining slats snapped. The next thing he knew, he, Ling, and the cub were falling.

12

By the time Michael, Chang, and Lei reached the foot bridge, the poachers were gone. Only Chu remained, sitting on the rocks, staring down at the turbulent water rushing through the ravine. Michael stopped beside him, wondering what the old man was staring at.

"Where are they, Chu?" Michael asked. "What happened?"

With a sluggish movement filled with sorrow, the old man pointed at the bridge, which now had huge gaps between the remaining slats. Then he gestured down at the water and muttered something in Chinese.

"The river?" Michael guessed.

Chu nodded. Michael felt a panicked jolt rage through him. They'd fallen off the bridge! There was no sign of his son or Ling. Could they have possibly survived? It didn't seem likely, but the alternative was too dreadful to even consider.

"Come on!" Michael yelled, starting out along

the top of the ravine and following it downriver. "We have to look for them."

Hobbling on his bad leg, Michael led the others along the river. The roar of the water drowned out almost all other sounds, but at one point he thought he heard Ling's voice.

"Stop!" He held out his hands toward the others. "Did you hear that?"

The others stopped and listened. Michael saw the frowns on their faces.

"I thought I heard Ling," Michael explained.

The Chinese men glanced at each other. Chu mumbled something and they nodded.

"What did he say?" Michael asked.

Lei shook his head. "Nothing."

Chu mumbled something more sadly.

"What's he saying?" Michael asked.

Chang and Lei glanced at each other, clearly reluctant to speak.

"Come on," Michael insisted. "Tell me."

"Chu does not think the children survived the fall," Lei said, unable to meet Michael's gaze.

Michael closed his eyes and felt as if he'd been stricken. No, he thought, that can't be true.

Ryan felt cold. Something hard was pressing against his stomach. Something soft and mushy pressed against one side of his face. A roaring sound was in his ears. Ryan opened his eyes. A reflex action suddenly made him gag and cough.

His mouth filled with water and he spit it out.

For a moment he was completely disoriented. What happened? Where was he? Seeing the river rushing past just a few feet away brought back the memory of floundering helplessly in the turbulent water, of being flung downriver and banging into rocks.

How he wound up lying on the rocky riverbank with his face in the mud, he'd never know. Something nudged him. Ryan turned sideways and found the panda cub looking at him, its fur matted down and wet. Nearby was Ling's day pack. Ryan picked it up and looked inside. He found the white leather collar they'd put on Chih. A lot of good that would do him, he thought, tossing it onto the shore.

"Ryan!"

Ryan looked up and saw Ling hurrying toward him with a huge look of relief on her face.

"Are you all right?" she asked, kneeling down next to him and the cub.

"Uh, I think so," Ryan replied, surprised that she seemed to care so much. Ling must have realized that she'd let her guard down, because her face grew hard.

"You let go of me!" she said angrily. "I told you I can't swim. I almost drowned!"

"That makes two of us," Ryan replied. "But I didn't let go. Not until the water pulled us apart."

Ling grabbed her pack away from him and

started to rummage through it. She took out some soggy tissues and a wet-looking Milky Way bar.

"The meat sticks are gone," she said sadly. "All that is left is the candy bar."

Ryan suddenly realized he was starving. "Split it with you?"

"No, we'll save it for an emergency," Ling said.

"What do you call this?" Ryan asked.

The panda cub crept close to Ling and sniffed at the candy bar.

"The cub is hungry, too," Ling said.

"Hey, I got first dibs," Ryan said. His stomach growled and churned hungrily.

Ling stood up. "The cub doesn't eat candy."

Ryan got up and looked around. "So how are we going to get back?"

Ling looked back up the river for a few moments before answering. "I'm not sure how far downriver we've come. If we can find Siguniang, we're okay."

"Siguniang?" Ryan repeated.

"It means 'four sisters,' " Ling explained. Just then her eyes went wide and she ran over to the water's edge and picked up the white collar Ryan had tossed away. She examined it closely and spoke excitedly in Chinese.

"English, please," Ryan said.

"This radio collar is for tracking pandas," Ling said. She squatted down and started to fiddle with the electronic tracking device.

Ryan stepped closer. "What are you doing?"

"Trying to start it," Ling said. "Maybe the battery is loose."

Ryan reached for the collar. "Let me try."

"No, I'll do it," Ling said. "If the collar is working, they'll find us."

But Ryan wouldn't give it back. Ling glowered at him.

"You don't know what to do," she said.

"Relax," Ryan said as he pressed down on the battery screw and turned it with his thumb. "I'm an American. My life revolves around electronics. Believe me, I can handle this."

The words were hardly out of his mouth when the screw opened and the battery popped out and promptly fell into the water where it was swept away. Ryan couldn't believe it.

Ling turned livid. "You are a moron!" snapped angrily. "Now they won't be able to find us."

Ryan tucked the panda collar into his belt. "What makes you so sure they're still looking?" he asked. He was still amazed that they'd both survived their ride down the river. He would have bet anything that most people would have drowned. Surely that possibility must have crossed his father's mind. But apparently it hadn't crossed Ling's mind.

"Of course they're looking." She gave him a

76

reproachful glare. "Grandfather will be very up-
set."

"At least somebody'll care," Ryan said with a
shrug.

Ling gave him a curious look. "You think grandfather would abandon me? You think Dr. Tyler
would abandon you?"

"It wouldn't be the first time," Ryan said bit-
terly.

Ling shook her head. "You don't know what you
are talking about. Your father is a good friend to
the people here. He's a good friend to the pandas."

"That's the problem," Ryan said. "He was too
busy being everyone's friend. Everyone but mine.
I mean, why wasn't he in the stands when I was
playing Little League and hit that triple? Why
didn't he come to the emergency room when I
broke my arm? Why didn't he come to Career Day
with all the other fathers?"

It just poured out of him. All that built-up re-
sentment and anger. And now Ryan could feel
tears threatening to follow. He turned away.
"Let's just get out of here, okay?"

"How's your batting average?" Ling asked behind him.

"Huh?" Ryan turned back. Was she being sar-
castic?

"Your batting average," she said.

"Uh, two fifty," Ryan said. "But the season just
started."

"Still, it's better than last year," Ling said.

Ryan scowled at her. That was right, but how did *she* know?

"Your father read your letters to me," Ling explained. "He read everyone your letters. He's very proud of you."

"You serious?" Ryan asked.

Ling nodded. "Be nice to your father. He is the only one you've got."

13

Chang led the other men along the riverbank. He monitored the tracking antenna that was supposed to pick up the signals from the panda collar.

"Is it picking up anything?" Michael asked.

Lei said something to Chang in Chinese. Chang shook his head.

"No," Lei said. "No signal."

"I don't get it," Michael said, mostly to himself. "I know Ling had the radio collar. I saw her take it off Chih and put it in her backpack."

Chu spoke in Chinese.

"Chu said the sun is setting," Lei said. "We must leave now and come back tomorrow morning."

"I can't leave," Michael said. "Not until we find them."

"We can't find them at night," Lei said. "We have no flashlight, no food."

"But I can't go back knowing they might be out there somewhere," Michael said.

"There's nothing we can do," Lei said, shaking his head. "We must wait until morning and then we'll come back."

Michael hated to admit it, but he knew Lei was right. Together with the other men, they returned to the helicopter and headed home. Behind them, the sun turned red over the mountain peaks and went down. Michael spent the entire trip wondering what the odds of finding Ryan and Ling alive again were.

Arriving back at the reserve, he turned his attention to other matters. Chih had recovered enough to be put in one of the outdoor enclosures and he wanted to see how she was doing. He found her inside a large, comfortable cage.

"Hi, girl." He waved. Chih didn't respond. Her rear paw was heavily bandaged and she appeared to be depressed, no doubt over losing her cub.

A worker came by, pushing a wheelbarrow filled with green bamboo leaves and stalks. He opened Chih's cage and put a bunch inside. The panda didn't make a move.

"Come on, girl," Michael said. He picked up a leafy shoot and placed it close to the panda, but Chih still wouldn't touch it.

"She's not eating," the worker said.

Michael nodded and picked up another shoot, pressing it toward Chih. "You have to eat, Chih.

You have to be strong for your cub when he comes back."

Chih didn't touch the bamboo. Michael put it down with a disheartened sigh. The truth was, he couldn't blame her.

Chang came by with a bowl of rice and handed it to Michael. "You should eat, too."

"Thanks." Michael took the bowl and Chang left. Michael looked down at the rice and realized he had no appetite either. It seemed like he and Chih were in the same situation — both wondering if they'd ever see their children again.

As night fell, it started to rain. Ryan, Ling, and the cub sought shelter in the hollowed-out trunk of a large old tree. Space was cramped and they sat in the dark with their legs pulled up under their chins. Outside the raindrops splattered on the leaves above and dripped to the ground. The cub made soft, crying sounds.

"Sounds like he's hungry," Ryan said.

"He's crying," said Ling. "Want to hear a story?"

"Sure," Ryan said with a shrug. "It's not like I can go in the next room and turn on the TV."

Ling picked up the cub and hugged it. "A long time ago, the panda bear was all white. One panda had a friend, a young girl. She was the youngest of four sisters. Every day this panda helped the girl herd her father's sheep. The panda and the girl were best friends. One day a leopard came. It wanted to eat the panda. The girl tried to stop the leopard, and she was killed."

"So this is a sad story, huh?" Ryan guessed.

Ling nodded. "The girl's three sisters made a funeral by the river. Pandas came from every part of China. To honor the girl, all the pandas rubbed black ash onto their arms. It's a sign of mourning."

"Yeah, like athletes do," Ryan said. "They sew a black stripe on their uniforms."

"The funeral was very sad," Ling went on. "All the pandas cried. They hugged each other to share the sorrow. The black ash got on their white fur. They cried so much, all the pandas rubbed tears from their eyes. The ash got into their eyes. When the pandas opened their eyes again, the three sisters were all gone."

"Wha . . . ?" Ryan had sort of lost the story.

"The three sisters missed their dead sister so much they jumped into river," Ling explained. "At the bottom of the river they joined hands. The next day a mountain rose out of the river. It had four peaks."

"The Four Sisters?" Ryan guessed.

"Yes," said Ling. "They stand guard over pandas, watch over them, protect them forever."

"And that's why pandas are black and white today?" Ryan said.

"The pandas never forgot the girl who cared so much, so they stayed black and white," said Ling.

Ryan could see that Ling was really caught up in this fairy-tale stuff. He truly hated to burst her bubble. "Sorry, but you and I both know that's bull."

Ling's eyebrows rose in irritation. "Grandfather does not lie."

"If these four sisters are real, then how come the panda is going extinct?" Ryan asked.

Ling had no answer to that. She only gazed at the ground and shook her head sadly.

The rain started to come down harder, splattering and rattling against the leaves above. Ling looked up.

"Lucky we found a tree," she said.

"No. Lucky would be finding a motel with MTV," said Ryan. He shifted around, trying to get comfortable but only managed to bang his head against a bump in the tree. "Ow! Stupid tree!"

Ryan made a fist and hit the tree in frustration, but that only made his hand hurt. "Darn it!"

Ling smiled.

"What're you smiling at?" Ryan snapped.

Ling didn't answer. Ryan's stomach rumbled emptily.

"Boy, I'd do anything right now for a Big Mac and fries and a chocolate shake and then a hot fudge sundae," he said. Then he remembered something. "Hey, where's the Milky Way?"

Ling shook her head. "No, we must save it."

"For what?" Ryan asked. "I'm hungry, I'm tired, I'm soaking wet, and I'm freezing."

"But we saved the cub," Ling said.

"Big deal," Ryan muttered. "What's that got to do with anything?"

"You think the world revolves around you," Ling said accusingly. "You don't even care about the panda."

Ryan crossed his arms. "If those poachers had shot the cub on the bridge today, we wouldn't be sitting in a tree right now."

"The poachers did not shoot at the cub," Ling said. "They were shooting at us."

"Us?" Ryan was shocked.

"Yes."

"They can't shoot us," Ryan said indignantly. "We're just kids."

"There's a strict law in China," Ling said. "The panda is very important. If you kill a panda, the punishment is very severe."

"Yeah, right. How severe?"

"The punishment is death," Ling said.

"I'll say that's severe," Ryan said. "Remember those two panda skins in the cave? Those guys could face the death penalty."

Ling nodded. "So they have nothing left to lose."

Ryan nodded. He hadn't thought of it that way. "I can't believe we're risking our lives for one stinkin' little panda."

"The cub is very important," Ling informed him.

"Uh-huh." Ryan nodded dubiously.

"The committee will vote to keep the reserve open another year only if we have a healthy cub," Ling explained.

"What do you mean?" Ryan asked.

"The committee will close the reserve if we have no cub to show them," Ling said with a yawn.

Ryan gazed out at the rain. "So if we get the cub back in time, then the reserve will have to stay open and my dad'll have to stay in China for another year."

Ling didn't answer. Ryan saw that her head was bowed and she'd fallen asleep with the cub in her arms. Ryan knew what he had to do, but he'd wait until morning to do it.

14

Ryan slept for a few hours. When he woke, the sky was just starting to go from dark to gray. The forest was quiet, the air heavy and damp. Ling was still fast asleep. The cub had hardly budged. Ryan felt stiff. He crawled out of the trunk and stretched. His breath came out in a misty white plume and he felt a chill. Knowing he couldn't dawdle, he scooped up the panda cub in his arms and headed into the woods.

He also brought with him something he hadn't expected, a strong feeling of guilt.

"Look," he said to the panda, cradled in his arms as he walked, "it's not my fault. If I help Ling bring you back to the reserve then I won't get to see my father for another whole year."

Ryan stopped at a grassy patch of ground where the rising red sun managed to peek through the trees. He put the panda down.

"You're better off out here in the wild," he said.

"If you came back with us you'd probably spend the rest of your life in a cage. Believe me, I'm doing you a big favor."

The cub looked around helplessly. Ryan's sense of guilt grew stronger. Deep inside, he knew he wanted the panda to go for his selfish reasons. He reached for a piece of bamboo and broke it off, handing it to the cub.

"Here's a little snack for the road," he said. "You can't follow me. You have to stay here. Go out and make some friends."

The cub stared at the bamboo and then dropped it and started toward Ryan.

"Oh, no." Ryan backed away. "You stay here."

The cub kept following him.

"Go on!" Ryan yelled at him. "Get lost!"

He ran behind a tree and waited to see what the cub would do. The cub looked around, then sat down and started to whimper. He looked so innocent and defenseless. Oh, no, don't do this to me, Ryan thought.

The cub continued to whimper. Ryan felt a pang deep in his heart. He knew he couldn't leave that little thing alone in the forest. If something bad happened to it, he'd live with the guilt for the rest of his life. Besides, that panda had never done anything bad to anyone. It had never tried to hurt anyone. It didn't deserve to have anything bad happen to it.

Ryan came out from behind the tree and started toward the cub. As soon as the panda saw him, it looked happier.

"If you weren't so little and cute this wouldn't be so hard," Ryan said. The cub climbed up on his leg and clung to him. Ryan rolled his eyes. "I can't believe I'm talking to a panda."

When Ryan returned to the hollowed-out tree, Ling was up. She gave him a quizzical look and Ryan made up some excuse about going for a walk. Ling and he started off into the forest again. The cub stayed clinging to Ryan's leg.

"I think it likes you," Ling said with a smile.

"I can't shake it," Ryan said, shaking his leg a little and smiling back. He hated to say it, but he'd actually started to grow fond of the little critter.

A short while later, Ling stopped and pointed ahead. Through the tree trunks Ryan caught a glimpse of the river. Unlike the ravine, the river was wide, flat, and slow-moving at this spot.

"Look, we can cross the river here," Ling said, reaching down to pull the cub off Ryan's leg. As she did, she saw the white leather collar Ryan carried tucked into his belt.

"Why do you have that?" Ling asked.

"It might be my only souvenir from this trip," Ryan said with a shrug.

They started toward the river. Its banks were covered with broad, moss-covered rocks. Ryan could hardly get any traction on the moss. It was sort of like trying to walk on ice.

"Kind of slippery," he mumbled, holding his hands out for balance as he tried to step over them.

"Yikes!" Next to him, Ling lost her footing and grabbed for his arm.

"Whoa!" Ryan was no help. He instantly fell down with her. The next thing he knew, the two of them were sliding down over the moss-covered rocks. The moss was so thick it cushioned the rocks, and the ride was almost fun until Ryan heard a rumbling sound that grew louder and louder.

"What the . . . ?" Ryan's eyes widened. They were sliding right toward a waterfall. "Oh, no!"

He tried to find something to grab onto, but couldn't. Everything was covered by that slippery moss. A second later they slid off the rocks beside the waterfall.

They weren't airborne for long.

Splash! Plop! Ryan landed in something soft, wet, and sort of gucky. He sat up and opened his eyes. He was sitting in a shallow pond filled with slimy greenish ooze. The pond sat next to the river, at the bottom of the waterfall. He was covered with green slime. Ling sat up next to him. She was covered with it, too. They both started to wipe it off their faces.

Something rubbed against Ryan's leg.

"*Ahh!*" he shouted and jumped to his feet. Looking down he saw that it was the cub, also covered with gunk. Ling laughed. Ryan felt humiliated.

"Ha-ha, very funny," he snapped, feeling his face burn. "If you want to see something funny, you should look at your face. There's stuff all over it."

"There's stuff on your face, too," Ling said, pointing back at him. She touched something on her face and her expression instantly changed.

"Leeches!" she screamed, and quickly started wiping them off her face. Ryan reached up and felt them on him, too.

In a reflex action, they both started to pull the little bloodsucking creatures off.

Finally, Ryan was certain he'd gotten them all off. Breathing a sigh of relief, he looked over at Ling, and realized they were both still covered with muck.

Splash! Splash! They both had the same idea and ran to the river and jumped in. The water was chilly, but refreshing. At least it helped get the rest of the slime off. Once in the river, Ryan looked over at Ling to make sure she was all right.

Now they both stood in the river with the water up to their shoulders. The panda cub sat on the shore and watched them with a curious expression. But it wasn't long before Ryan started to shiver. The water was cold and his teeth had started to chatter so he jumped out and raced to shore. Ling was shivering, too.

"Ling, it's starting to get cold," he said.

"I'm not cold," Ling said.

"Gimme a break," Ryan said. "I can see you shivering from here. Why do you do that?"

"Do what?" Ling asked.

"Act like you're so tough."

"I am tough." Ling jutted her chin out.

"Maybe, but you're allowed to have a little fun every once in a while," Ryan said.

"There's no time for fun," Ling said. "I'm busy with the pandas."

"But you're just a kid," Ryan said. "Don't you ever want to go to the mall with your friends and play video games?"

"Mall?" Ling's forehead wrinkled.

"Yeah, it's a bunch of stores all together."

"And this is fun?"

"Sure."

"I have no time for friends," Ling said. "I must earn money to help my family."

"Why?" asked Ryan. "Where's your dad?"

"My father is dead."

Ryan hadn't expected that. It caught him off guard. "Oh . . . I'm sorry."

"My mother and little sister are in Chengdu," Ling went on. "Dr. Tyler spoke to the Chinese government so I could have a job in the reserve with grandfather."

"My dad did that for you?" Ryan asked, surprised.

Ling nodded. "My mother is very happy because now she's not worried that I am without family. So I am grateful to *your* father."

Now Ling looked directly at him. "You are very lucky to have a father."

Ryan was starting to see his father in a different light. Maybe she was right.

Chih still wouldn't eat. Michael stepped into her cage and offered her a fresh shoot of bamboo, but the large panda just glanced at it and looked away. Michael slid down the wall to the floor and ran his hand through his hair.

"You must really hate us, huh?" he said.

Chih gave him a curious look, as if she wanted him to explain.

"The bad guys took your cub from you," Michael said, "and the good guys locked you up in this jail so you can't go out and find it. Makes no sense does it?"

Chih held him steadily with her eyes.

"At least you did everything you could to show your cub how much you love it," Michael said. "Me, on the other hand . . ."

The words trailed off. Michael took a deep breath and sighed.

"When Ryan was smaller, he and I went on this camping trip," he said. "It was just the two of us

92

and we did a lot of fishing. Ryan hooked a sixteen-inch bass. I swear, the fish was almost as heavy as he was. He fought that monster for half an hour. At least a dozen times I thought he was gonna quit. I kept asking him if he wanted me to take over, but he insisted that he could catch that fish by himself.

"Well, he finally landed it and we must've laughed and hollered for an hour. I'll tell you, my son fighting that fish by himself for so long . . . he was so brave . . . a lot braver than me."

Michael stared down at the floor for a moment, then looked back up at the mother panda. "I'm a coward, Chih. I put my work ahead of my family, ahead of my son. And then I didn't have the guts to face him and own up to it."

He shook his head slowly. "That's why I hardly answered any of Ryan's letters. I didn't know what to tell him. I figured I'd talk to him in person when he came here" — he could feel his eyes start to fill with tears — "and now he's out there somewhere lost, maybe even dead. And I may never get the chance."

15

Ryan had just spent the last hour sitting on the shore, telling Ling about American TV and *Gilligan's Island*. And what Ling called, "The Bunch of Bradys."

Just then his watch beeped. *American Gladiators*, he thought. Too bad there was no TV . . .

Wait a minute! His watch!

It had a battery!

Why hadn't he thought of it before? Ryan jumped up and detached the radio collar from his belt. Sitting down next to Ling and the cub, he turned the collar around and opened the battery compartment.

"I can take the battery out of the wristwatch and put it in the collar," Ryan said.

"Careful," Ling cautioned him.

Ryan snapped the battery into the collar. "Got it!"

A red light in the collar started to blink.

"It worked!" Ling cried out with joy.

Ryan held up one hand and gave himself a high-five with the other. "Ryan, my dude, you are a genius!"

The sleeplessness of the past few days had caught up to Michael. He'd fallen asleep in Chih's cage. Suddenly someone was shouting his name and jabbering at him in excited Chinese. Michael opened his eyes. It was Chang, gesturing to him eagerly to follow.

Michael climbed out of the enclosure and followed Chang into the tracking room. Still half asleep, Michael couldn't understand why Chang was pointing at a blinking red light on the tracking board with such excitement. Then he realized that the light was coming from an area downriver from the ravine.

"Ryan!" he gasped under his breath.

Chang nodded. Somehow the kids had gotten the tracking device to work again. Michael quickly found Lei and Chu in their rooms and told them.

A little while later Lei brought the old tractor around with the trailer hitched to it. Michael climbed on board and they started to head into the forest. All at once they heard shouting coming from behind. Looking back, they saw Chu running toward them, waving.

Chu ran up to the tractor and spoke with great

urgency to Lei, who turned to Michael.

"He wants to go with you," Lei said. "He says Ling and Ryan are his children also."

Michael smiled and nodded. Lei climbed down off the tractor and Chu climbed up. Once again the tractor started off into the woods.

Ryan and Ling had covered a lot of ground. They were no longer in the mountain forests. Now they were on the edge of a broad valley with terraced farm fields green with corn. Ryan carried the cub. The radio collar was still tucked under his belt. The cub seemed a little listless.

"Ling, you think it's okay?" Ryan asked.

"It needs mother's milk," Ling said. "The cub cannot go long without it."

"Neither can we," said Ryan, whose stomach felt like it was permanently cramped. "I'm starved."

Without warning, the cub squirmed out of his arms and got free. Before Ryan could grab it, the baby panda scampered off into a field of corn.

"Hey, come back here!" Ryan shouted as he and Ling chased it.

Ryan and Ling banged through the corn stalks. Unlike the stiff bamboo, these gave way easily. Suddenly, Ryan looked up and froze. A man wearing a colorful robe and a turban was standing in the field, glaring at him.

"Uh, Ling?" Ryan said in a voice that was barely more than a whisper.

As Ling joined Ryan, the man started to scold them in an angry voice.

Ryan glanced nervously at Ling. "What's he saying?"

"I can't tell," Ling replied. "He speaks Tibetan, not Chinese."

"Can't you understand any of it?" Ryan whispered.

"A little," Ling replied. "He seems mad."

Ryan rolled his eyes. Like he couldn't see that for himself? "Thanks for the insight," he groaned.

Just then the cub decided to return, and sat down at Ryan's feet. The Tibetan man stopped talking and looked down. The next thing Ryan knew, the man was smiling from ear to ear. He said something more in Tibetan and then gestured for them to follow him.

"What do you think?" Ryan asked Ling.

"I think we should do what he says," Ling said.

He led them toward a village of small huts made of mud and stone and covered with thatch roofs. Everyone who saw them stopped and stared, first at the panda, then at Ryan. He had the feeling that for these people, seeing a Western boy was as rare as seeing a panda.

In the center of the village, the man stopped and waited while an older man came toward them.

He was wearing brightly colored robes and a hat lined with dark fur. His face was as wrinkled as a prune and his hair was almost white. He stopped a few feet from Ryan and scrutinized him severely. Ryan felt uneasy and bowed.

"So, uh, how's it going?" he asked.

Instead of answering, the older man reached out toward the cub. Ryan backed up slightly, uncertain why the old man wanted him, and unwilling to give the little animal up. The old man muttered something and Ling turned to Ryan.

"It's okay," she said. "He will not hurt the cub."

Ryan handed the cub over and the old man smiled broadly. Other villagers crowded toward him and petted the cub gently.

"Good news," Ling said. "The cub is, how do you say it — our meal ticket?"

She was right. The village hastily prepared a festive meal for them. The bad news was what the meal was comprised of.

They sat outdoors at a rough wooden table. A small Tibetan boy sat next to Ryan, watching his every move with wide fascinated eyes. Ling teased Ryan about having a new friend.

The men at the table held up glasses filled with rice wine in a toast and the old man spoke. When he was finished, Ryan looked to Ling for a translation.

"I think he said that we are friends because we protect the panda," Ling said.

They passed food around, dropping wooden spoonfuls of it on Ryan's plate. Ryan was so hungry he hardly cared what it was. He just wanted to eat. Around him the villagers' chopsticks clacked rapidly as they devoured the food. Ryan picked up his chopsticks and tried to get them to work, but the food kept falling off them. The people around him smiled knowingly.

"Here." Ling placed her hands on his. Ryan felt goose bumps run up his arm when she touched him. "This one keep still. Only move this one."

Ryan did as she instructed and actually got some food into his mouth. He chewed it happily. It had an unusual flavor. He turned to Ling. "What is this stuff?"

"Monkey brain."

Ryan stopped chewing and felt the blood drain out of his face. He pointed his chopstick at the other foods on his plate. "What about this?"

"Steamed fungus in red chili with pepper and fresh yak milk," Ling said.

Fungus? Athlete's foot was a fungus. Ryan was starting to feel a little queasy. He pointed at something else. "Please say this is chocolate."

"Slugs," Ling said.

Ryan started to lower his chopsticks. He might have been starving to death, but there was no way he. . . . Then he noticed that everyone else at the table had stopped eating, too. They were all looking at him with worried expressions on their faces. Ryan didn't want them to feel like they'd failed him. He picked up the chopsticks and started to chew again. The others smiled and returned to their own meals.

Ryan leaned toward Ling and spoke in a whisper. "I hate to tell you this, but this isn't real Chinese food."

"No?" Ling looked surprised.

"Where are the egg rolls?" Ryan asked. "Where's the wonton soup? I don't even see a fortune cookie."

Ling looked at him like he was crazy. Ryan sighed. It occurred to him that she had no idea what he was talking about.

16

After the dinner they tried to get the cub to eat, but it was obvious the little panda only wanted its mother's milk. By then the sun was setting and it became apparent that the Tibetans expected Ling and Ryan to spend the night. They would have to continue their journey to the panda reserve in the morning.

The old man led them to a large barnlike building. Inside were big wooden bins filled with grain, as well as a tall pile of firewood and some old wooden carts. Nearby, sacks filled with potatoes were stacked against the wall. The old man pointed at a loft above them. A layer of straw was spread over the floor of the loft, and some flat, empty sacks were spread on top of it. The old man spoke and Ryan got the feeling he was telling them that this was where they were going to spend the night.

They climbed a wooden ladder up to the loft. The empty sacks laid out over the straw actually made for a half-decent mattress. Then again, just about anything would be better than sleeping in a hollowed-out tree trunk again.

"Well, at least the accommodations are improving," Ryan said, looking around.

Ling was watching the cub, who was weak from lack of nourishment and looked as limp as a rag doll.

"Tomorrow it may be too late," she said sadly.

Ryan looked down at the furry black and white creature. He remembered reading that all animals grow fastest soon after birth and that was when they needed the most nourishment. But the cub hadn't eaten in days.

Then he had an idea. "Wait here." He climbed back down the wooden ladder and ran back to the site of the dinner. Some Tibetan people were cleaning up, and Ryan gestured to them until they understood what he needed.

A little while later he returned to the loft carrying a rice wine bottle filled with fresh yak milk. He'd rigged a piece of cloth over the opening, hoping it would work like a nipple.

"What is it?" Ling looked delighted, but also puzzled.

"Yak milk," Ryan explained. "I know it's not panda milk, but it might work."

Ling placed the bottle at the cub's mouth. The cub opened its mouth to taste the milk. Ling and Ryan shared a silent look of hope.

The cub turned away. Ling offered the bottle again, but it was obvious the panda wasn't going to take it. Ryan slumped down, disappointed. Then he felt Ling touch his shoulder gently.

"It was a good idea," she said sadly. He could tell she was sincere.

They laid down on the sacks. Ryan expected to fall asleep quickly and was surprised some time later to find himself lying on his back, wide awake. Not far from him, Ling appeared to be fast asleep. Ryan sat up and decided to go outside. Maybe the fresh night air would help him feel sleepy.

He climbed quietly down the ladder and walked out of the barn. The night sky was truly amazing. You had to be really far from city lights, and pretty high above sea level to see such an incredible sight. He'd never seen so many stars! There were literally millions of them up there. The thickest concentration was almost directly overhead in the Milky Way, which Ryan had never seen so clearly before.

Then he felt something nuzzle his leg. Looking down, he saw the panda cub.

"Hey, you." He bent down and picked the cub up, then looked up at the stars again. "Know what? We gotta come up with a name for you."

Ryan pointed up at the sky. "See all those stars? I know almost every constellation up there. My dad painted 'em on my bedroom ceiling. He said that if I ever get lonely, I could look up at them and no matter where he was, we could be looking up at the same thing. That way we'd never be apart."

Ryan looked down at the panda, who gazed back at him with its dark eyes.

"There's even a constellation named after you," Ryan said, pointing up again. "There it is. The Little Bear. You're safe up in the sky. No poachers can get you up there."

He heard footsteps. Ling was coming toward him in the dark.

"It's an old custom in my country when a baby is born to bring him under the stars and give him a name," she said. "That way, the evil spirits know he is from heaven. What name do you like?"

Ryan smiled. "Well, the panda is a cub, and the greatest Cub who ever lived was Ernie Banks."

Ling shook her head. "I don't like Ernie Banks for a cub. How about a Chinese name like Ssu-ma Yang Hsuang-ju?"

Ryan shook his head. It was too hard to pronounce. "I have this friend back home. He's sort of short and fat and his name's Johnny. How about we call the cub Johnny?"

"Jah-Ni," Ling said. "In my language that means 'best in the forest.'"

"Yeah, well, my friend wouldn't be best in the forest," Ryan said. "Maybe best in the lunchroom, but that would be about it."

"I like the name," Ling said. "From now on, the cub is Jah-Ni."

"Okay, now we better get some sleep," Ryan said.

They started to walk back to the barn. Ryan noticed that Ling was studying him.

"Tell me, Ryan," she said. "When you go to a mall, do many girls want to go with you?"

It was an opportunity for Ryan to make her believe he was a big stud, but his heart wasn't in it.

"Well, not really," Ryan said. "To tell you the truth, I'm not really a big ladies' man."

"Oh." Ling nodded and they walked along in silence. Just before they reached the barn, she looked up at him again. "Maybe someday I'll visit America. Then will you take me to a mall?"

Ryan couldn't help smiling. "Yeah, sure."

17

Ryan felt a hand clamp down over his mouth. His eyes burst open. He was lying on a sack in the barn. It was light outside. Ryan stared up into the wrinkled, weathered face of the old Tibetan man. The man whispered something harshly.

"Huh?" Ryan didn't know what was going on.

The old man removed his hand from Ryan's mouth and pulled him to a window. Outside Ryan saw two men carrying rifles and looking around. The poachers! He quickly turned back to the loft and shook Ling until she woke up.

"The poachers are here!" he hissed.

Ling's eyes widened. "They must not see Jah-Ni!"

Ryan looked back at the old man. "How're we gonna get out of here?"

The old man nodded calmly as if he understood exactly what Ryan had asked. He gazed around and then pointed at the sacks filled with potatoes. It seemed to Ryan that he was getting an idea.

A little while later, Ryan, Ling, and the cub were hiding in rough potato sacks in the back of a cart. The sacks around them were filled with potatoes. Ryan could smell the horse that was in the process of pulling the cart out of the barn. Outside sunlight filtered in through the sack. The cart stopped. Ryan heard gruff voices questioning the old man. The voices must've belonged to the poachers. The old man's answer sounded short and innocent.

Ryan prayed the poachers would move on, but he could still hear them mumbling. Meanwhile, Jah-Ni was scratching around in his sack, trying to get out.

One of the poachers said something, and while Ryan couldn't understand Chinese, he was willing to bet it was "What was that sound?"

The old man muttered something and the cart suddenly lurched forward. Good, Ryan thought. Now he heard the voices of children. It sounded as if a group of them were walking alongside the cart. Just then a commotion began among the children. Ryan had a feeling it had something to do with Jah-Ni. He poked his head out of the potato sack.

Oh, no! Jah-Ni had gotten out of his sack!

The kids were crowding around the back of the cart, trying to shoo the little cub back into his sack. Looking in the other direction, Ryan saw the poachers watching curiously.

Suddenly, the cub jumped off the cart!

Darn! Ryan pulled himself out of the potato sack and jumped off the cart, too. He scooped up Jah-Ni and hopped back on. The poachers pointed at him and started to run.

"Move this thing!" Ryan shouted.

The old man had been leading the horse on foot. Now he spun around and saw the poachers running toward them. He whacked the horse on the rear and the cart started to pick up speed and bounce along. Meanwhile, Ling squirmed in her potato sack.

"I cannot get out!" she shouted.

Ryan bent down and started to untie her sack. The cart was bouncing around so much that it was hard for him to keep his hands on the cords holding the sack closed. Meanwhile, the younger poacher, Po, was getting closer and closer to the cart. Before Ryan could stop him, he reached out and grabbed the back of the cart!

Ryan shoved a sack of potatoes off the back of the cart with his foot.

"Oooof!" Po tripped over the sack and fell.

"Untie me!" Ling cried.

Ryan got back to work. "I'm trying!" he shouted.

The horse was galloping at full speed and they were bouncing all over the place. Ryan finally managed to get the sack untied.

"Here!" he yelled, and pulled it down over Ling's shoulders.

Ling started to fight her way out of the sack. Ryan looked around to see where they were going. Just then he noticed that the horse was running about twenty yards to their left!

The harness had pulled loose! There was nothing guiding the runaway cart! They were headed away from the farmlands and back into the woods!

"Hold on!" Ryan shouted.

They must've hit some kind of bump, because the next thing Ryan knew, they were airborne.

Crash! The cart hit the ground and rolled. Ryan felt himself flung and tossed around . . . like a sack of potatoes.

Then, amazingly, he was lying on the ground and nothing hurt. The cart lay upside down nearby, one of its wheels squeaking as it continued to turn.

The cub crawled out from under the cart. Ling followed, looking dazed.

"You okay?" Ryan asked.

Ling nodded.

"And Jah-Ni?"

Ling nodded again and looked up past him with surprise in her eyes. Ryan turned. Behind him in the distance stood a mountain with four rocky peaks rising majestically into the air. Ryan immediately knew what it was.

"The Four Sisters," he said in awe. "Cool."

The moment was interrupted by a little cough and a wheeze. Ling and Ryan looked down at the cub.

"Jah-Ni sounds sick," Ling said.

Ryan picked up the cub and rose to his feet, staring off toward the mountain. "How far are we?"

"The reserve is on the other side of the mountain," Ling said. "It'll take two days. Maybe more to go around."

Ryan looked down at the cub. "I don't think we have that much time. Why can't we take a shortcut and go over the mountain?"

Ling shook her head. "It's much too dangerous. The passages are very narrow and very steep. There's a lot of fog. Many people have tried to go through and they're never seen again."

The cub wheezed again. Its eyes were glassy and unfocused. Ryan had a bad feeling. "Ling, Jah-Ni may be dying. I don't think we have a choice."

When the trail grew too steep, Chu and Michael left the tractor behind and continued on foot. Chu carried the tracking device and glanced at it occasionally, trying to follow Ryan's path. Suddenly he stopped and looked very worried.

"What is it?" Michael asked.

Chu said something in Chinese. After two years in China, part of it sounded vaguely familiar to Michael.

"Say it again," he said.

Chu repeated himself more slowly this time. Michael winced and felt a nauseated sensation in the pit of his stomach. There was no doubting what the old man had said. Ryan and Ling were trying to cross the Four Sisters.

18

The tops of the peaks were encased in a misty gray fog as thick as pea soup. Below, Ryan and Ling climbed along the side of a rocky cliff. Old, spindly pine trees grew here and there on the cliff. Some had fallen over, others had roots sticking straight out into the air.

Ling carried Jah-Ni. Ryan carried a thick piece of bamboo about the size of a baseball bat. At one point Ryan stopped and licked his finger, then held it in the air.

"How does your grandfather do this?" he asked.

Ling stopped behind him. She looked tired. "Ryan, I cannot climb anymore. The cub is too heavy."

Ryan went back and kneeled beside her. "Come on, we can't give up now. It can't be much further."

Ling rested the cub on a rock. The cub looked skinny and weak. It laid its head on the cold stone.

"It's no use," Ling said wearily. "Jah-Ni can't

even hold his head up. We'll never make it in time."

Ryan knew how easy it would be to give up, but Ling's doubts seemed to give him strength.

"Listen up, Ling," he said. "Remember the bridge? Remember when I wouldn't let you go. Jah-Ni is not going to die. I'm not going to let him."

Ling looked up hopefully at him.

"I promise," Ryan said, holding out his hand to her.

Ling hesitated for a second, then grabbed his hand. Ryan pulled her up to her feet. They both looked down at the cub.

"I have an idea how to carry him," Ryan said. "Give me your day pack."

A few moments later they pressed forward with Jah-Ni in the day pack on Ryan's back. They inched their way along the rocky cliff, in and out of the old trees. At one point the thick mist parted and Ryan caught a glimpse of green hillsides, a cascading waterfall and a blue river below . . . *far* below.

Until that moment, he'd had no idea how high up he was. Please, Four Sisters, he thought to himself, don't let me fall. Your job is to take care of pandas. Me, too. I'm on your side.

They continued slowly. At one point a rock under Ling's foot gave way and hurtled downward. Ryan grabbed her hand and steadied her.

"Careful," he said.

They came to a tall, rocky ledge and followed it. For a while it was too high to see over. Then it dipped for a moment. Ryan looked over.

"I can see the other side," he cried happily. "Hang on, everyone. It won't be long now."

He continued along the ledge. It stopped up ahead. Ryan knew all he had to do was turn the corner and . . .

Suddenly he froze. Ling came up behind him.

"Why did you stop?" she asked.

"Look," Ryan said, pointing ahead where the ledge ended and clear empty air began. Ryan felt his heart sink. "It just ends. There's nowhere to go."

"Then we'll go back," Ling said.

"No," Ryan said. "There's no time."

He looked past her and saw something that made his jaw drop. The poachers were right behind them! Ling must have seen his face because she turned and saw the poachers, too.

Ryan quickly looked around but there was no way to escape. Ahead the ledge ended. Behind they walked right into the hands of the poachers.

The older poacher, Shong, came close and reached out with one hand and said something.

"He wants Jah-Ni," Ling said.

"Well, he's not getting him," Ryan said.

The poacher must have understood because he rushed forward and tried to grab the day pack.

114

"No!" Ryan fought back, grabbing Shong by the shoulders.

Shong still managed to get the cub out of the day pack and hand it to Po. Ryan now jumped on Po, grabbing for the cub.

"Give him back!" he shouted.

Ling jumped on Po, too. The younger poacher stumbled and fell to the ledge. The three of them rolled close to the edge, fighting for Jah-Ni. Shong stood over them, trying to pull Ling off.

Ryan remembered his bamboo bat and rolled away. Grabbing it, he jumped up and swung at Po's knee.

Wham! The man cried out in pain and grabbed his knee.

"Strike one!" Ryan shouted gleefully, and swung at Po's other knee.

Bam! The poacher grabbed his other knee and crumbled to the ground, letting go of Jah-Ni. The panda rolled away and came to a stop on the edge.

Ling dove for the panda cub. Shong tried to stop her. Ryan couldn't believe the fight Ling put up, but the poacher finally got hold of her. It looked as if he was going to throw her off the ledge!

"Ryan!" she screamed. "Help!"

Ryan ran toward her, but Po managed to tackle him and bring him down.

"Leave her alone!" Ryan shouted as he struggled to get out of the younger poacher's grasp.

Ling grabbed a tree root and held on for dear life. Shong started to pry her fingers off one by one. Just when it looked like he'd succeeded, Ryan suddenly heard a voice shout, "Ling!"

Someone swung around the ledge through the air, hanging from a rope. Ryan couldn't believe his eyes. It was his father! Pulling a stunt that would have made Indiana Jones proud!

"Dad!" Ryan shouted.

Shong spun around.

Whomp! Michael punched him in the face. The poacher staggered backward and collapsed on the ledge.

Meanwhile, Po snatched the cub and started to scamper up the side of the mountain peak.

"He's getting away!" Ryan cried and started after him. He grabbed Po's leg. Po tried to shake him off, but only managed to lose his balance. Suddenly all three of them — Po, Ryan, and Jah-Ni — tumbled back down.

Thunk! Po hit the rock ledge hard and was knocked out. Ryan grabbed a rock and broke his fall. But then he watched in horror as the cub rolled past him and toward the ledge.

"Jah-Ni!" Ryan cried.

A second later the ball of black and white fur rolled off the ledge and vanished!

"No!" Ling screamed. She and Ryan shared a look of horror. Then Ryan dashed to the ledge and looked over.

Wait! Jah-Ni was there! Hanging from a thick tree branch that jutted out of the rocks just below the ledge. Without a second thought, Ryan slid over the ledge to the branch.

"Ryan!" his father cried from above.

The branch felt pretty solid. Jah-Ni was clinging to it about five feet away. It had to be at least a two-thousand-foot drop straight down from the branch to the green forest below. Ryan stood on the branch and held his arms out for balance. He could feel the emptiness around him. Except for the branch, there was nothing but air . . . thin air.

Slowly, carefully, he inched his way out toward the panda cub.

"Ryan, come back here!" his father shouted. "That branch can't support you!"

Ryan didn't listen. He'd come too far and had gone through too much to let this poor little creature perish now. The only thing that mattered was saving him.

Don't look down, Ryan told himself. He inched out farther on the branch, aware that there was nothing but air beneath him for thousands of feet. Out in the sky, almost at the same height as Ryan, an eagle swooped and soared. He could feel every bump and twist in the branch as his feet slid over it. Jah-Ni stared up at Ryan with that innocent look in its eyes.

"Ryan, please don't!" Ling gasped behind him.

Ooops! Ryan's foot suddenly slipped on a loose piece of bark. *Whoa!* He waved his arms desperately in an attempt to keep his balance.

"Oh, no . . ." his father groaned behind him.

But Ryan managed to regain his balance. Once again, he started toward the panda cub.

"It's all right, Jah-Ni," he said softly. "I'm coming."

Creak. . . . The branch sagged a little as Ryan stepped farther out. He was almost close enough now. Ryan smiled.

"Hi, Jah-Ni." Ryan held out his hand. The panda cub reached toward him with one paw.

Crack! Without warning, the part of the branch holding Jah-Ni suddenly snapped! Ryan lunged forward and grabbed the cub, practically out of midair, and saved him from falling. Then he staggered back and sat down on the branch, cradling the little creature in his arms while he caught his breath and waited for his heart to stop pounding.

A huge wave of relief swept through Ryan. Behind him, he could hear Ling and his father let out big sighs. Ryan hugged the panda and buried his face in the animal's fur. Everything was going to be okay.

Finally.

CRRRACK! Ryan felt a sudden jolt as the branch under him began to give way!

"Ryan!" his father cried out. "Hurry!"

Holding the cub with one arm, Ryan lunged

back toward the ledge, reaching out toward his father. It didn't seem possible that he could make it. Chu appeared, having taken the long away around. When he saw what was happening, he grabbed Ling and shielded her eyes from the sight of Ryan falling.

SNAP! Just as the branch broke, Ryan reached out. His father grabbed his hand and yanked him onto the ledge. Michael's face was filled with a fury born of sheer terror.

"You could have been killed!" he screamed at his son. But a second later he hugged him for joy.

19

The tractor bounced and rattled as it rolled back down the side of the mountain. Chu was driving like a maniac. Michael sat beside him along with Ling and Ryan, who still held Jah-Ni in his arms. The two poachers were tied to the trailer behind them.

As they reached the valley, they could see the panda reserve in the distance. A group of men in dark suits was climbing into a minivan.

"It's the committee!" Ling cried. "They're leaving!"

As the tractor roared closer, the van started to pull away. Chu spun the tractor's wheel, cutting the van off and hitting the brakes. Ryan, Ling, and Jah-Ni tumbled off. In the minivan, the men in suits were jolted forward. The door opened and they got off the bus, shouting angrily in Chinese.

Michael climbed down from the tractor and headed toward Mr. Hsu.

"Dr. Tyler," Hsu sputtered. "What is the meaning of this?"

"I'm sorry," Ryan's father apologized, "but we couldn't let you go without — "

"Too late." Hsu cut him short. "The decision to close the reserve has been made."

Michael's brow creased. "Close the reserve?"

"Yes," Hsu said. "You have not bred any pandas. Not even one cub."

"But you don't understand," Michael started to say.

Mr. Hsu was no longer listening. He was staring past Michael at Ryan, who walked over to them carrying Jah-Ni. The committee began to "ooh" and "ahh" as they crowded around Ryan.

"Uh, sorry," Ryan pushed through them and headed toward the buildings. "I've got a special delivery to make."

Ryan hurried toward Chih's enclosure and everyone else followed. Ryan heard Mr. Hsu say something about keeping the reserve open for another year. As they neared the mother panda's cage, they could see Chih sitting listlessly inside. A fresh pile of bamboo on the ground near her lay untouched.

Ryan pulled open the door and placed Jah-Ni on the floor of the enclosure. Then he and the others stepped back and watched. Chih looked down at the cub and began to whimper. Then, with a grimace, she pulled herself onto her feet

121

and limped toward the cub. Jah-Ni, so weak he could hardly move, dragged himself toward his mother.

When Chih was close enough, she reached out with her paw and drew her cub in. Jah-Ni cuddled against his mother and immediately began to nurse.

Ryan felt his eyes well up. The tears fell out and rolled down his cheeks. He felt someone come close to him and turned to find Ling. Her eyes were also filled with tears. Behind her Chu stood with a beaming smile on his leathery face. The old man said something in Chinese.

"Grandfather wants to thank you for keeping his granddaughter safe," Ling said. "And saving the panda."

Chu bowed at Ryan, who bowed back. "You're welcome."

With his face still wet with tears, Ryan licked his finger and held it in the air.

"Would you ask him how he can tell things by his finger?" he asked Ling.

Chu must have understood because he laughed. Then he whispered in Ling's ear.

"He said it's very simple," Ling said with a big grin. "He licks his finger, then it becomes wet. So he holds it up in the air to dry."

Ryan rolled his eyes, knowing that wasn't the truth, but that it was probably the closest he was going to get. The old man walked away. Ling leaned toward Ryan and kissed him on the cheek.

"I take back what I said. You are very brave, like your father."

Ryan felt his face turn red.

"I had a fun time," Ling added. "Thank you."

Michael came over and put his hand on his son's shoulder.

"You think the cub will be okay?" Ryan asked.

"Yes," his father said. "But we still have a problem."

"What?"

"We're going to have to keep Chih and Jah-Ni here for a few months until the cub has his strength back and Chih's paw recovers," Michael said. "Things are going to be so busy around here that they may not get all the attention they need."

"Can't you hire somebody?" Ryan asked.

"I suppose we could." Michael rubbed his chin. "Just out of curiosity, have any plans for the summer?"

Ryan's eyes went wide. "Mean it?"

"You bet," Michael said with a smile.

Ryan hugged his father. He couldn't think of a better way to spend the summer.

About the Author

TODD STRASSER has written many award-winning novels for young and teenage readers. Among his best-known books are *Help! I'm Trapped in My Teacher's Body* and *Help! I'm Trapped in the First Day of School*. He speaks frequently at schools about the craft of writing and conducts writing workshops for young people.